CRAVING THE COWBOY'S KISS

ROWDY RANCH

Vicki Lewis Thompson

Ocean Dance Press

Visit the author's website at
VickiLewisThompson.com

"You know what? We probably shouldn't be talking about this."

Oh, so he wasn't unaffected. Gratifying. But she'd be wise not to look at him. So much for wisdom. She had to know. Sure enough, Gil's eyes had turned that sultry navy blue that gave her butterflies.

Did he want a do-over?

Faye's heart began to pound. What did *she* want? She'd better get clear on that, because right now she was a captive of her hormones.

If he invited her into his bedroom, if he promised her that he'd wipe that crummy first impression right out of her brain and body with one, maybe two spectacular orgasms, could she resist? Stupid question.

His gaze remained steady but his breathing was not. "I'm guessing from the way you're looking at me, you know what I'm thinking."

"Doesn't take a genius."

"Just because I'm thinking it doesn't make it a good idea. We have a wedding to attend next weekend and I'm sure you want it to be the best day ever. For all concerned."

"Of course."

"So do I. Going back to my bedroom to try and fix the past might work. But it might blow up in our faces."

*Want more cowboys? Check out these other titles by
Vicki Lewis Thompson*

Rowdy Ranch
Having the Cowboy's Baby
Stoking the Cowboy's Fire
Testing the Cowboy's Resolve
Rocking the Cowboy's Christmas
Roping the Cowboy's Heart
Tempting the Cowboy's Sister
Craving the Cowboy's Kiss

The Buckskin Brotherhood
Sweet-Talking Cowboy
Big-Hearted Cowboy
Baby-Daddy Cowboy
True-Blue Cowboy
Strong-Willed Cowboy
Secret-Santa Cowboy
Stand-Up Cowboy
Single-Dad Cowboy
Marriage-Minded Cowboy
Gift-Giving Cowboy

The McGavin Brothers
A Cowboy's Strength
A Cowboy's Honor
A Cowboy's Return
A Cowboy's Heart
A Cowboy's Courage
A Cowboy's Christmas
A Cowboy's Kiss
A Cowboy's Luck
A Cowboy's Charm

A Cowboy's Challenge
A Cowboy's Baby
A Cowboy's Holiday
A Cowboy's Choice
A Cowboy's Worth
A Cowboy's Destiny
A Cowboy's Secret
A Cowboy's Homecoming

Sons of Chance
What a Cowboy Wants
A Cowboy's Temptation
Claimed by the Cowboy
Should've Been a Cowboy
Cowboy Up
Cowboys Like Us
It's Christmas, Cowboy
Count on a Cowboy
The Way to a Cowboy's Heart
Trust in a Cowboy
Only a Cowboy Will Do
Wild About the Cowboy
Cowboys and Angels

1

Worst party ever. Gil McLintock's cheeks hurt from fake smiling. Evidently he'd produced a convincing display of good cheer, though. Not a single member of his loving, boisterous family had guessed his nerves twanged like freshly strung barbed wire.

And why should they guess? They were too busy focusing on the happy couple. His brother Marsh and Ella Bradley were getting married next Saturday and they'd decided to skip the traditional bachelor and bachelorette parties.

Instead, they'd invited family and friends to a big bash at Rowdy Roost, the saloon-styled rec room his mom had added last year. Everyone in attendance was over the moon about this marriage.

That included him. Marsh and Ella belonged together. No problem there.

But as for Ella's sister Faye... big problem. He hadn't been in the same room with her for more than a year, but nothing had changed since the last time.

Prior to this gathering he'd convinced himself she'd act differently towards him now that the official family connection was days away. No such luck.

As usual, she'd treated him as if he'd had a recent run-in with a skunk. The generous square footage of Rowdy Roost gave her plenty of room to maneuver. She'd kept a minimum fifteen-yard distance.

She had to be tracking his every move just as he was tracking hers. He'd tested it by edging in her direction several times. She'd always shifted away. Subtly. Never making direct eye contact.

Yeah, he could just ignore the situation. Except they'd be rubbing elbows next weekend whether she liked it or not. With the dinner Friday night, the ceremony on Saturday and the reception at the Buffalo, they'd be in each other's space constantly.

Would anyone notice her behavior? Maybe not. But they were in for years of forced togetherness and eventually someone would remark on it. Ask questions. The story would come out.

He wanted to get ahead of that. Logically she should want the same thing—to talk this out and diffuse the tension. But they needed to do it soon and the discussion required privacy.

In conversation with Ella, he'd discovered Faye had come here with her folks. Guaranteed Ella and her parents knew nothing about the incident ten years ago. They all treated him like a cherished member of this new family combination.

Faye's transportation choice offered up a plan. A half-assed plan, but it was better than allowing this nonsense to continue. He'd ambush her when the party ended, which should be anytime now.

His mom traditionally stationed herself in the entry to bid each guest goodbye. Her collie Sam loved this routine. By standing next to her, he collected extra doses of affection.

Consequently, the exodus took a while. That could work to his advantage.

Locating Rance, he explained he wouldn't be staying to play pool, after all. Then he worked hard not to fidget while the room gradually emptied out. The front door remained open on this warm August night, adding to the leisurely pace of the farewells.

When the Bradley contingent finally headed toward his mother and Sam, Faye dropped back and let her parents go first.

Gil managed to keep clear of Faye's peripheral vision as he closed in. She looked nice tonight. He hadn't been this close to her since the last time he'd tried to coax her into a conversation about their predicament.

She'd let her hair grow longer since then, which showed off the natural wave as it curled around her shoulders. His fingers remembered the silky texture of it.

She'd worn a fancy turquoise western shirt that matched her boots. Her shoulders were relaxed. She had no idea he was there. A whiff of her spicy perfume stirred a memory. A hot one. *Not helpful, dude.*

While Faye's mom chatted with his mom and Gerald Bradley loved on Sam, Gil considered his options. A tap on her shoulder? No. Should he clear his throat? Lame. Face it, he'd scare her no matter what he did. Couldn't be helped.

"Faye."

She whirled around, eyes wide, mouth open. Her cheeks turned pink and she pressed a protective hand to her chest. "*Gil.* You about gave me a heart attack." The words came out in a breathless whisper.

"I apologize." He kept his voice down. "Listen, I have something of yours. I think you'd like to have it back."

"What?" She swallowed.

"It's—"

"Never mind. Just give it to me."

"It's not here."

"Why not?" Suspicion clouded her gray eyes.

"Because giving it to you here would be… awkward." And he hadn't finalized his plan until fifteen minutes ago. "Listen, let me drive you back to town. We'll stop at my cabin on the way and pick it up."

"No, thanks." Suspicion turned to panic. "Throw it away."

"My conscience won't let me." And he'd have to find it, first. Best guess, it was in his underwear drawer.

"What could possibly—"

"It's personal."

"Good Lord." Her voice lowered to a soft murmur. "Is it from that night?"

"Related to it."

Her color deepened. "I was so drunk."

"So was I. Look—"

"Okay, okay." She held up her hand like a traffic cop. "Don't make a scene. I'll come with you." Her parents were saying their final goodbyes as she turned back to his mom. "Great party, Ms. McLintock. Thank you so much."

"Hey, we're going to be related. Call me Desiree."

"I'd be happy to... Desiree."

"There. Was that so hard?"

"I can't say it was easy. You've been Ms. McLintock my whole life. But I'll work on it."

"Good. I'm glad you could make it tonight. Seems like ages since I've seen you."

"The UM theatre department keeps me pretty busy."

"I believe you. It's just that you used to be out here all the time when you, Ella and Marsh were kids. I miss that. You three were such good buddies."

"We were. Still are, but things—"

"Change. I know. I'd love it if you'd stop by more often, though."

"I'll do my best. Anyway, you'll be seeing a lot of me next weekend."

"Looking forward to it."

"Me, too." After a quick smile, she hurried outside to join her parents.

"I'll be right there, Faye," Gil called after her.

His mom's eyebrows lifted. "What do you mean, *right there?* You're leaving, too?"

"Yes, ma'am."

"I thought you and Rance—"

"I'm giving Faye a ride back to town."

"Didn't she come with Liz and Gerald?"

"Yes, but I need to talk to her about something."

"And you didn't manage that during the party?"

"It's...private."

"I see."

His mother had questions. Questions he wasn't about to answer. Not now, anyway. "And it's complicated."

"Obviously."

"I'll fill you in later." Maybe. So much depended on Faye. He walked out to the porch and caught the tail end of her explanation to her folks. Something about high school memorabilia.

Her father, aka Doc Bradley to everyone in town, switched his focus from his daughter to Gil. "Isn't that out of your way, son?"

"It's no bother, sir. I need to make the trip this weekend, anyway, so might as well do it now. I need to check on something at the metalworks shop." Just making it up as he went along.

"We'll stop by his cabin and pick up whatever he thinks is so *valuable*." She rolled her eyes. "Won't take long. I'll see you back home soon."

"Don't rush." Liz linked arms with her husband and started down the steps. "I'll bet it has something to do with the musical you two starred in."

His breath caught. "You're good, Mrs. Bradley." Did she know more than he thought she did?

Faye gave him a sharp glance. "Is it?"

"I guess you could say that."

She opened her mouth, closed it again and looked away.

Her mom looked over her shoulder. "To think that was ten years ago. Shouldn't you be having your class reunion soon?"

"It's in October." Gil walked beside Faye, who stayed out of touching distance as they followed her parents out to the parking area. "Same weekend as homecoming." Another reason to get this settled. He'd attended the five-year but Faye had been a no-show. Had he been the reason? That would suck.

"I have a soft spot in my heart for ten-year reunions. That's when Gerald and I reconnected."

"You and the doc graduated from Wagon Train High? I don't think I knew that."

"Sure did." Doc Bradley gave his wife a fond glance. "Coming up on the fortieth."

"Did you date each other back then?"

"No." He chuckled. "Because I was an idiot. Didn't ask her out. That reunion gave me a much-appreciated second chance."

"I wasn't very bright at eighteen, either." He snuck a peek at Faye to see if that might change her stoic expression. It didn't.

Her folks had parked farther from the house than he had so his truck came up first. He paused. "This is mine."

"I know. See you soon, Mom and Dad!"

She recognized his truck? While he was still absorbing that factoid, she scurried to the passenger side, hopped in the cab and closed the door with a solid *thunk.*

He headed for the driver's side. Well, of course she recognized his truck. It had the McLintock Metalworks sign on both front doors. Except in the dark, approaching from the back with vehicles on either side, the signs weren't visible. His personalized plate was, though, the one that said IRNMAN.

Climbing in, he inhaled her spicy scent. Again. "You're wearing the same perfume."

"You remember that?"

"Apparently so." And it was the tip of the iceberg. He'd been driving a different truck ten years ago, but having her in the passenger seat of this one created a tsunami of potent memories that shocked the hell out of him. Aroused him, too. Inconvenient.

"Is this thing you want to return an item from *Grease*?"

"Yes."

"Then what's the mystery? Why not tell me what it is?"

Because he wasn't sure he could lay his hands on it. "I'd rather surprise you."

"Because if you told me, I might not care about it. You're just using it as an excuse to—"

"Finally have a conversation about this ridiculous situation? What if I am?"

"I *knew* it. I can still catch my folks." She unbuckled her seatbelt.

"Faye, don't leave." He was sorely tempted to hit the lock button. But he was better than that.

"Just let it go, okay? I—"

"Please. We need to talk."

She hesitated, her hand on the door handle, not looking at him, her jaw set. "Talking won't change anything and might make it worse."

"Speaking for myself, it can't get worse. Family gatherings are supposed to be joyful. Did you have fun tonight?"

"Sure."

"Oh, really? Ready to sign up for more of that next weekend?"

She sighed, let go of the door and fastened her seatbelt. "All *right*. We'll talk, but not in your cabin. I don't want whatever souvenir you've squirreled away. We can conduct this discussion you're so hell-bent on having on the way to town."

"That won't work for me." He buckled up and started the truck.

"Why not? I know for a fact you can talk and drive at the same time."

"Because we should be face-to-face." He pulled away from the house and turned left at the main ranch road.

"I take it your cabin's in the opposite direction from town?"

"Yes, ma'am."

"Which means we're not stopping on the way like you said."

"Small detail. It's just down the road. Three or four minutes."

"How about we just park in front of it and have this conversation in the truck? If you insist on seeing my face, you can switch on the dome light."

"Not what I had in mind. I'll make coffee. We'll sit across from each other at my kitchen table while we hash this out."

"You make it sound like a diplomatic mission."

"Exactly!" He smacked the steering wheel. "Couldn't have said it better myself."

She settled back in the seat with another deep sigh.

When she didn't offer any more comments, he kept his mouth shut, too. He had plenty to say, but he'd wait until they were settled inside. Nothing broke the silence except the deep hum of the truck's engine and the crackle of the tires on the dry spots in the road, or the swish when he drove through a puddle left by the early evening rain.

"Was trying out for *Grease* your idea or Mrs. Allred's?"

Her question startled him. "Hers." She'd begged him to do it and he hadn't been able to turn down a nice teacher like Mrs. Allred.

It was his own damn fault that she'd found out he could sing. He'd been goofing around in the hall between classes, entertaining his buddies with a lame tune that was popular and making fun of the lyrics. She'd happened along.

"I'm not surprised that she asked you. It didn't really make sense that it was your decision."

"Why not?"

"You weren't in choir or drama. You were a jock. Did you hate doing it?"

"It felt weird at first. I'd never done anything like that before. But eventually I had fun with it." Especially in the scenes that had involved kissing Sandy, aka Faye Bradley. A few short weeks later, the memory of those tempting kisses had led to... yeah, the most embarrassing night of his life.

2

Gil's breathing had changed. Did dredging up the past make him anxious, too? That offered Faye a wee bit of comfort.

He'd been the coolest guy in their class. Too cool for her, but she'd admired him from afar. Then her drama teacher had recruited him to play Danny.

She'd suspected he'd been talked into it. But she hadn't asked, preferring to believe he'd suddenly discovered his creative side. If his surprise appearance at tryouts had been his idea, they'd finally have something in common.

She'd never have wished a broken leg on the boy Mrs. Allred had intended for the role of Danny. But Tony Marino's unfortunate accident had put Faye in the enviable position of kissing class heartthrob Gil McLintock instead. Turned out he had a talent for it. That much had been no surprise at all.

With plenty of gel in his hair, its reddish-brown color darkened enough to fit the part, and he'd already possessed the necessary muscles and swagger. Once he'd donned the black leather jacket, he'd become Danny.

That alone would have made her swoon. When she'd discovered he could sing *and* dance, she'd fallen hard. His kisses had sealed the deal. They weren't fake. He liked her. In her teen fantasy, like would turn to love and—

"Here we are."

Her nostalgia bubble burst as he turned off the engine and opened his door. "Let me help you down. The rain probably left some muddy patches."

"That's okay. I can get out on my own." Quickly unbuckling, she opened her door and stepped out on the running board. The truck's dome light revealed a glossy chocolate swath right where she needed to step. Maybe she could leap over it. But if she missed....

She'd worn her best dancing boots, too. Oh, well. Holding onto the door for balance, she put one foot down. Ugh.

"Don't say I didn't warn you." He stood a few feet away, arms folded, hat pushed back.

"I knew this whole thing was a bad idea."

"I could have lifted you over that and saved those fancy boots."

"Or you could have parked where it wasn't muddy."

"That's a guessing game in the dark. Not much to be done now. You're committed. Might as well treat the other one to the same fate."

She winced at the squishing noise as her left foot settled into the ooze.

"It's just mud, though. It'll clean off."

Yes, and she could use the mud to her advantage. "I'm not about to walk into your house in these boots." They made a sucking sound as she approached him. "Let's sit on the porch steps. That's good enough. If you'll fetch me a rag, I'll clean my boots while we talk so I won't get mud in your truck."

"How about I clean your boots as a goodwill gesture after we have coffee and a nice chat in the kitchen?"

"What's with the emphasis on coffee? For all you know I don't even drink—"

"You brought a thermos of coffee to rehearsals while the rest of us drank soda. You don't just *like* it. It's your favorite beverage."

So he'd remembered that. So what? "It's late to be drinking coffee."

"Not for you. Caffeine doesn't keep you awake."

Okay, one more detail he'd retained. She didn't want to be charmed but he... was charming, damn it.

"I have some of Marybeth's chocolate chip cookies." He said it with a smile.

Of course he had cookies. Marybeth adored the McLintock kids as if they were her flesh and blood. They'd all moved into places of their own, but that hadn't stopped her from baking treats and dropping them off now and then. Ella counted that among the many perks of living out at Rowdy Ranch.

Faye sighed. "You drive a hard bargain."

"You'll come in?"

"Yes. I miss those cookies."

"If we can iron out our differences, you could stop depriving yourself."

She rolled her eyes and set off. The porch light allowed her to avoid the muddy places and stomping her feet shook off some of the glop. When she reached the steps, she turned around and sat on the second one. "I'm taking these off so I don't track mud onto your porch."

"Okay." He paused beside her. "Need help?"

"No, thanks." She didn't want his charming self that close. Besides, she'd worn her lucky pig socks, the ones she put on to ward off stage fright. If he didn't get involved in removing her boots, he might not notice her socks.

She struggled to toe them off so she wouldn't have to touch the muddy part, but her pig socks had a grip on those boots. She'd have to reach down and grab the heel, which meant at least one hand would end up a mess.

Then she'd have to dirty up his kitchen sink. This gig was becoming more uncomfortable by the second.

"Let me." He crouched, a bandana in his hand. Before she could take a breath to protest, he'd neatly removed her left boot and set it next to the steps. "Are those the same lucky pig socks?"

Damn. He'd remembered. "No. Those wore out." She breathed in his achingly familiar aftershave.

"They look the same." He tugged off the right one, folded up the bandana and left it next to the boots. "Do I give you stage fright?"

"Don't be silly. I just—"

"It's not silly." He stayed where he was, his gaze level with hers. "It's a brilliant idea. I bought myself some crazy socks after you told me your trick."

"You did?"

"Still have 'em for emergencies. I just hate thinking you need lucky pig socks whenever I'm around."

"That's not why I—"

"Faye."

She sucked in a breath. The intensity of those electric blue eyes had made her heart go wild whenever he'd moved in close for a kissing scene. Her heart hadn't forgotten its automatic response to Gil McLintock.

As the rapid beat echoed in her ears, his eyes darkened to navy, exactly as they had before each memorable kiss.

He swallowed. His lips parted slightly.

Was he going to kiss her? Should she let him? No! *Yes.*

He stood abruptly and moved back. "Thanks for agreeing to come here tonight." He sounded hoarse. Cleared his throat. "Clearly it wasn't an easy decision."

"Um, no."

"Well, I appreciate it. Anyway, we should go in. That coffee's not going to make itself." He stuffed his hands in his pockets.

Evidently he wasn't going to help her up, which was contrary to his usual perfect manners. Was he worried that if he took her hand, it would lead to something they'd both regret? A shiver ran down her spine.

Grasping the railing, she pulled herself to her feet. "Coffee *can* make itself. You just need to sync your coffeepot to your phone."

"I'm assuming you've done that?"

"Of course."

He nodded as he started up the steps. "Sounds like you."

She wished he'd quit saying stuff like that, as if he knew her, as if he'd thought about her over the years.

He opened the unlocked front door. Everyone left their doors unlocked on Rowdy Ranch. Safest place in the world. At least regarding crime. Not so safe for her heart.

After motioning her ahead of him, he followed her in and closed the door.

The click of the latch unnerved her. It put an exclamation point on her current situation — alone with Gil for the first time since that fateful night ten years ago.

He'd billed this episode as a chance for a friendly chat. Maybe he'd believed that when he'd proposed it, but the scorching look he'd given her after he'd taken off her boots had little to do with friendship. Then he'd deliberately avoided helping her up.

Which meant he was aware of the chemistry, but clearly didn't want to go there. Neither did she. She'd had a moment of weakness when she'd wanted him to kiss her, but she'd be a fool to go down that road again.

Sensual ripples still flowed between them, though, especially now that she was standing in his house. Home ownership added a layer of maturity to Gil that... yeah, she found sexy. Unfortunately.

Light from a table lamp bathed the living room in a soft glow that revealed cushy furniture, a rock fireplace, and evidence of his metalworking skills. Stacked firewood nestled in a graceful wrought-iron holder on the hearth. The lamp's base was fashioned from horseshoes.

"This is nice."

"Thanks." He took off his Stetson and hung it on a horseshoe rack by the door. "Come on in the kitchen and have a seat while I make coffee the old-fashioned way." He headed toward an arched doorway on the left and flicked on the light.

She padded toward the kitchen, the honey-colored floorboards tempting her to pick up speed and slide in her pig socks. She liked the feel of this house, liked it way too much.

She reached the doorway at the same moment he turned on the coffee grinder. The noise covered her involuntary gasp of delight. If she had the money to design her own kitchen, it would look like this one.

Warm yellow walls highlighted the gold tones in the granite countertops and contrasted with cabinets painted Montana sky blue. She loved the mix of colors, but more than that, she loved the finish on all the edges.

Every single one, from countertop to cabinet door, was rounded and smooth, so inviting she wanted to stroke them. If a kitchen could be seductive, this one qualified.

He dumped ground coffee in the basket with a practiced hand. "I pestered Vern at the

Buffalo to tell me where he got this blend." He poured in water and tucked the carafe under the drip basket. "It should taste familiar." He glanced toward her and blinked. "Are you okay?"

"I'm dazzled."

"By Vern's coffee? It's good, but not—"

"The kitchen. I've never seen one so beautiful."

He smiled. "Me, either, except in a magazine. This is where I spent most of the money. It's my favorite room in the house."

"Are you into cooking?"

"I am, now. I love being in here, so I look for reasons, which means learning to cook more than the basics Mom and Marybeth taught all of us."

"Yet Marybeth still brings you cookies?"

"They're from her recipe, but I made them. Tweaked the recipe a little, but don't tell her."

"I'm flabbergasted. I never would have guessed that you'd..." She waved a hand around the room. "Get excited about a kitchen."

"Why not?"

"Because... I guess because it doesn't fit my image of you."

"Which is?"

"Your license plate, of course. IRNMAN. You were a jock in school and now you're a blacksmith, which—"

"Farrier."

"Same thing. You work with heavy stuff. Hot stuff. Which takes a lot of muscles, which you have in abundance and—"

"You think I'm too manly to want a beautiful kitchen?"

She gulped. "Apparently not."

"Good thing I dragged you out here. Sounds like you've been avoiding some made-up muscle man instead of me. The jock from high school, maybe?"

"Maybe."

"That's who I was ten years ago. People change. How about we start over and find out who we are now? It sure would make family gatherings easier if we could be friends."

"It would." Except friends didn't look at friends the way he'd looked at her only minutes ago out by the porch steps. How did he plan to deal with that?

<u>**3**</u>

"Then it's decided. We'll work on becoming friends." Which could end up being way more complicated than Gil had expected. When he'd dreamed up this scheme for solving the issue, he hadn't factored in his attraction to Faye. Which was alive and well, damn it.

Evidently he'd been lying to himself about that attraction for years. Anytime a glimpse of her had prompted a zing of arousal, he'd shrugged it off as leftover vibes from the musical — Sandy and Danny, hormonal teenagers in love for the first time. A random blast of lust from the past.

But he was twenty-eight, for crying out loud. He should have outgrown that. Then tonight he'd looked into her eyes and the overwhelming urge to kiss her had blotted out all the reasons that it was a terrible idea.

Thank God he'd come to his senses just in time. He'd been seconds away from making a colossal mistake. Had he learned *nothing*?

News flash — *his brother was marrying her sister*. His stupid decision to have sex with Faye ten years ago had come back to bite him in the ass. It was time to mend fences, not set the corral on fire.

"So where are these cookies you keep talking about?"

"Right here." Picking up a ceramic jar in the shape of a giant mushroom, he brought it to the table and took off the gold and white spotted cap. "Cookies."

"If they taste as good as they smell…"

"Try one."

She reached in, snatched a cookie and took a generous bite. "Mmm."

"My thoughts, exactly." And there he was, staring at her mouth, a perfect cupid's bow paired with a temptingly plump lower lip that begged to be nibbled on. Plates. They needed plates and napkins. He went to fetch them.

"That was delicious."

"Thank you." He set the plates and napkins on the table and went to the cupboard above the coffee pot to grab two mugs. Her stage kisses had been delicious, too. Sweet, with an undercurrent of forbidden fruit. That undercurrent had been his downfall.

"The cookie jar fits into your color scheme."

"Can't take credit for that. Mom bought it for me." He glanced over at the coffeemaker, which had stopped gurgling. "Still take it black?"

"Sure do."

"Then pick a seat. I'll bring it to you."

"I like round tables." She picked up a plate and napkin before choosing the chair that gave her the best view of the kitchen.

"It was a no-brainer considering all the curved edges in here." After delivering the coffee, he sat across from her with his back to the array of cabinets and appliances.

"How did you end up with something like this?" She helped herself to two more cookies.

He pulled out three. They were excellent cookies if he did say so. "I saw a similar design in a magazine my mother had. That setup was totally out of my price range, but I kept looking online and eventually found this company. More reasonable, but still pricey. I had to scale back some of my other plans for the cabin."

"Did you ask Clint if he could do it?"

"I did." He sipped his coffee. "Be careful. It's hot."

"Just how I like it." She took a hefty swallow.

"Oh, yeah, I forgot. Never too hot for you."

"Nope. So what happened when you asked Clint? I hear he's gung-ho when it comes to woodworking projects."

"He said it would be a fun challenge, but when he told me how long it would take him to create this effect, I wasn't willing to wait."

"Why the rush?" She picked up another cookie.

"Bret and I had this race to see who would finish their cabin first. I was determined to beat him. You know, younger brother trying to outdo his older sibling."

"I know that game." She popped the last of the cookie in her tempting mouth and brushed crumbs from her fingers.

"Guess you would."

She finished chewing and swallowed. "Did you beat him?"

"By almost a week. I don't think he really cared, but I did."

"Sounds like me and Ella." She cradled her mug in both hands and took another drink. "This cabin thing you all have going amazes me. Everybody went for it. How come?"

"It's fun, for one thing. But also, Mom set the example. Her childhood wasn't all that stable, so owning a home was everything to her. She encouraged us to save for a place of our own, too."

"You must have had to start saving early."

"Yes, ma'am, although everyone still had to take out a loan, which Mom cosigned. She also deeded us each a parcel of land so that was one expense we didn't have."

"And nobody ever said no, thanks, I've decided to live somewhere else?"

"Why would we? This is home."

"You know that's unusual, right? Almost nobody stays put these days."

He laughed. "Might be true in Missoula. Not in Wagon Train. Almost all of us stay put."

"Except your dad. And the other dads."

"They don't count. They were only passing through. And they didn't buy real estate. Mom was right. Having my own place, even if it's not all paid for, gives me roots. Feels great, too."

"I can see that." She put down her coffee. "I've never experienced it. I saved money as a kid, but never with the idea of buying a *house*."

"But enough for a down payment?"

"That wasn't on my radar. I spent it on a trip through Europe to visit all the famous performance venues. I'm saving up to go again in a year or so."

"You talked about wanting to do that."

"I did? When?"

"Senior Ditch Day."

"Oh." She grabbed her mug and took a quick swallow. "Do you like to travel?"

"Dunno. Never had the extra cash for a trip. Besides my home loan, Bret and I took out a business loan so we could launch McLintock Metalworks. Until that's paid off, we'll both be watching our finances."

"That shop was a brainstorm. Your work is beautiful."

"That's Bret's doing. He's the artistic one in the—"

"Not the only one. A family in my old neighborhood has a wrought iron gate you made. They mentioned you by name."

"The Carvers?"

"Yep. They adore that gate. I can see why. The tree-of-life design is gorgeous."

"Thanks." Was he blushing? Sure felt like it. He could handle praise for his cookies. But Bret was the artist, not him. He was the marketing guy who schmoozed the customers, took the bulk of the farrier work and made stuff when he had time.

"I think you'd enjoy seeing Europe. You could check out what the artisans are doing in other countries."

"I wouldn't mind going over there, although Bret's the one who should—"

"Why aren't you willing to admit you're creative, too? Maybe you weren't into musical theater all that much, but—"

"I was into it."

"Okay, yeah, you said you had fun."

"That's my standard answer. The truth is I loved that experience. I loved it so hard."

She put down her half-eaten cookie and stared at him. "Really?"

"Yes, ma'am. But I've never told anyone. I'm not sure why I'm telling you."

"Why keep it a secret?"

"Because of Bret. By the time we were in junior high, we'd already decided to open a farrier business once I'd graduated from high school. But after the musical, I considered bailing on him."

"To go into acting?"

"Yep. I planned to use my savings to enroll at UM. Then I'd see where this acting thing would take me."

She sucked in a breath and let it out. "Wow."

"It would've been a bad move."

"You don't know that."

"Yes, I do. Danny was a great role for me and I didn't have to compete for it. I had a cushy situation with Mrs. Allred who gently gave me the training I needed to succeed in that setting. You tell me. Is that how it normally goes for a struggling actor?"

"No. I see your point."

"You get it because you know the business firsthand. I would have torpedoed the partnership with Bret, blown a chunk of money and likely quit when I finally discovered the job is way tougher than I'd thought. And I'd have to leave Wagon Train to have any shot at the big time. I'd ignored that aspect, too. I love it here."

"But you changed your mind. Why would it matter if Bret found out?"

"Because he wouldn't get it the way you do. I can picture him torturing himself, convinced I sacrificed a brilliant acting career to stay here and be his business partner."

"Your secret's safe with me. "

"I know it is. I can't believe you've never told Ella about that night."

"I can't believe you've never told Bret."

His conscience whapped him upside the head. "I haven't told Bret, or anyone, except—"

"Except who? Your mother?" Panic rose in her voice. "Dear God, I hope you didn't—"

"No, not Mom. I told Dallas."

"*Dallas*? Angie's guy?"

"I didn't identify you by name. Although in hindsight he may have figured that out."

"Why in the world would you tell Dallas something that you've never mentioned to any members of your family?"

"I was afraid he'd get sexually involved with Angie, and—"

"Which clearly he has, now! When did you tell him about us?"

"Before they had sex, but he ignored my advice not to go there."

"I don't get what Dallas and Angie have to do with—"

"It's the risk factor. He loves it here, loves this family. If he and Angie break up, it'll be... I don't know what it'll be. Not good, that's for sure."

"But isn't that true no matter which couple you're talking about?"

"Well, sure. But Dallas is more vulnerable than most. He's not from here and has no kin living in the area. I saw it as a potential mess for him. And for Angie, but more for him."

Faye sighed. "I can see that. And I'll admit that Marsh and Ella's marriage shines a spotlight on our family dynamics. Sooner or later someone will notice that we don't talk to each other and ask questions."

"Then why did you give me such a hard time about having this conversation?"

"Because I don't want to talk about it. That was the most embarrassing night of my life."

"Same here."

"Oh, I doubt that, Mr. High School Heartthrob. I was a virgin, but you—"

"So was I."

She gasped. "You *were*?"

"Yes, ma'am."

She stared at him, her color high, her breath coming fast. "That..." She gulped. "That changes everything."

<u>4</u>

If only she'd known. Faye's image of that night shifted like a Rorschach inkblot. The white vase became two silhouettes, hers and Gil's. "Why didn't you tell me?"

"Why didn't *you* tell *me*? I didn't figure it out until I met resistance." He sucked in a breath. "Then it was too late. I couldn't stop."

"You thought I had experience? How could you think that?"

"You just seemed... I don't know...*worldly.*"

"Me? Faye Bradley from Wagon Train?"

"You were never just Faye Bradley from Wagon Train. You were going to Europe so you could, as you put it, *fill the well* with all you'd see and do there. You said it would improve your craft. Your *craft.* No other girls I knew had that kind of focus."

"Since when does focus indicate sexual experience?"

"You acted like an adult, so I assumed—"

"Who did you *assume* I was having sex with?"

"Tony."

"Tony?" She couldn't help smiling.

"When you agreed to have sex with me, I decided you'd broken up with him, because you're not the type to—"

"Sex with Tony was never gonna happen."

"Why not? You were always hugging each other. Talking in whispers, laughing about something or other."

Had Gil been jealous? What a heady thought. "Yeah, we got along great. He keeps in touch."

"Are you saying there was nothing between you?"

She took pity on him. "Just friendship. He likes guys."

"Oh!" He blinked. "How about that? Huh."

"The truth is, I didn't date much in high school. But you were always going out with somebody or other. I find it hard to believe that you never—"

"Believe it. My mom didn't tell us not to have sex, but she warned us that when we did, even if we used condoms, there was always a chance we'd become parents."

"A small chance, though."

"True, but that comment made an impression. Whenever I was tempted, I asked myself if I'd be okay with her being the mother of my child. The answer was always no."

"Until me? Why would you take the risk with me? That makes no sense."

"Well, we were totally smashed. There was that."

"Are you saying you were too drunk to remember what your mother told you?"

"Actually, I wasn't. Mom's warning ran through my head that night, just like it always had when I was about to take off my pants."

"And yet you ignored it."

"Not really. Maybe the booze mellowed me out. In any case, I decided I'd be fine if you became the mother of my child."

"What?" She stared at him.

He gave a little shrug. "That's what happened."

"Definitely the booze talking. You had no idea if I'd be a good mother or a bad mother."

"Yes, I did."

"How?"

"I'd paid attention. You already knew what you wanted out of life. You were excited about what lay ahead, you had plans. You'd be an inspiring role model for him or her."

"Except I wouldn't have been because a baby would have torpedoed my life! Did you think about that?"

"No. Sorry. I was eighteen, selfish and horny. No girl should trust a guy that age. We're awful."

"Well, I didn't get pregnant, so I guess it doesn't matter."

"But if you had, I wouldn't have let our kid torpedo your life. I would have done everything in my power to keep that from happening."

"Out of guilt?"

"Out of fairness."

"That's nice to hear." And his casual use of the phrase *our kid* gave her shivers. She hadn't worried about getting pregnant since he'd used a condom and she hadn't been given the warning he had. But if a failed condom had thrown her into parenthood with Gil McLintock... there were worse things.

He heaved a sigh. "I've been feeling guilty for ten years, knowing that your first experience with sex was horrible and it was all my fault."

"It wasn't all your fault. It was as much my idea as yours. In fact, I'm positive I'm the one who suggested we leave the crowd and drive down by the creek."

"Yeah, but I'm the one who'd scored all that booze we drank once we got there."

"Did you expect we'd have sex?"

"Oh, yeah, but I thought you'd seduce me."

She laughed. "I thought *you'd* seduce *me*."

"No wonder we drank so much. We were each waiting for the other one to make a move."

"And then you finally did."

"It's a wonder I was still capable. Large amounts of alcohol aren't recommended if you're planning on hanky-panky."

"I'd heard that. I wondered if you'd have a problem, but nope." And for a few seconds, she'd relished the intimate connection. The twinge of pain hadn't bothered her much, and when that was over and he'd thrust deeper....

The vivid memory caused heat to settle in her core.

"Oh, I had a problem, all right. It's called premature ejaculation. I had the staying power of a gnat. And I deeply regret that whole episode. You deserved better your first time."

The conversation was having a panty-dampening effect on her, but he didn't seem the least bit flustered. How embarrassing if she was turned on and he wasn't.

She called on years of training and put on an act of total coolness. "You deserved better, too. If I'd been as experienced as you thought, I might have been able to do something to help."

"I doubt anything would have helped. You felt so damn good that I..." He paused, took a breath. "You know what? We probably shouldn't be talking about this."

Oh, so he wasn't unaffected. Gratifying. But she'd be wise not to look at him. So much for wisdom. She had to know. Sure enough, his eyes had turned that sultry navy blue that gave her butterflies.

Did he want a do-over?

Her heart began to pound. What did *she* want? She'd better get clear on that, because right now she was a captive of her hormones.

If he invited her into his bedroom, if he promised her that he'd wipe that crummy first impression right out of her brain and body with one, maybe two spectacular orgasms, could she resist? Stupid question.

His gaze remained steady but his breathing was not. "I'm guessing from the way you're looking at me, you know what I'm thinking."

"Doesn't take a genius."

"Just because I'm thinking it doesn't make it a good idea. I should follow my own advice, the advice I gave Dallas."

"That he didn't take."

"That's his business. This is mine. And yours. We have a wedding to attend next weekend and I'm sure you want it to be the best day ever. For all concerned."

"Of course."

"So do I. Going back to my bedroom to try and fix the past might work. But it might blow up in our faces."

"Agreed."

Taking a deep breath, he let it out slowly. "I'm not willing to take that risk." He hesitated. "Are you?"

"Not when you put it like that. Sounds selfish as hell."

He pushed back his chair. "Then it's time for me to take you home."

"Let's go." She stood, although she was still a little wobbly from a rush of adrenaline. An image of going back to his bedroom remained lodged in her head even though they'd decided against it.

He gestured toward the arched doorway. "After you."

She started to pick up her dishes.

"Just leave 'em."

His terse command told her he was fighting the same battle she was. What if she'd said she was okay with the risk? Would they be headed for the bedroom instead of his truck?

She didn't remember her boots until she stepped out on the porch.

"Hang on." He stepped around her and clattered down the steps. "I'll deal with 'em."

She waited while he knocked off the worst of the dried mud and brought them to her.

"You can sit in the chair." He gestured toward the nearest porch chair, an Adirondack.

Perched on it, she shoved her feet into her boots and walked with him over to the truck.

"I'll get your door." He reached across, opened the door so the dome light came on, revealing a smaller mud puddle. "Need help?"

"I've got this." She climbed in, avoiding the puddle.

As he settled into the driver's seat, his movements lacked the smooth precision of the trip out here. He fumbled with the keys, had trouble latching his seatbelt, muttered a soft curse and finally shoved it home.

She chose not to comment. If she'd had to drive, she wouldn't be doing any better. But now that they were in this fix, she had a question. Should she ask it? She glanced at his profile, his tight jaw. Not yet.

When they reached the paved road that would take them back to town, he sighed. "Thank you."

"For what?"

"Agreeing we shouldn't have sex."

"You made a strong case."

"It's the right decision."

"It's certainly the safest one."

"Yes, ma'am. We need to concentrate on Marsh and Ella."

"We do. And it's good we had this talk."

"Now we're on the same page."

"About that." She took a quick peek at him. Some of the tension was gone from his face and neck. Might as well voice her concerns. "What if we've traded one problem for another?"

<u>5</u>

Gil let out a groan of frustration. "Don't say that."

"Somebody had to. What if we've jumped from the frying pan into the fire?"

"We haven't." If he was feeling the heat, he didn't have to admit it. "We'll handle this." But Faye's tempting perfume messed with his concentration. "It won't be an issue when we're around other people. Next weekend we'll be in a crowd the whole time."

"We were in a crowd tonight and I spent the whole evening focused on you."

"And I was focused on you, but now that we've talked through some things—"

"You won't be thinking about sex the next time you see me? You won't lose track of conversations because you're wondering if I'm also thinking about—"

"I'll keep my focus where it belongs, on Marsh and Ella."

"How did that work out for you tonight?"

She had him there.

"Just because the relationship's changed doesn't mean it'll be less distracting. It could be more distracting than ever. And possibly draw attention."

A headache worked its way up the back of his neck to the base of his skull. "Let's say you're right. What do you propose we do about it?"

"I'm not sure, but we need to find a strategy before the rehearsal and rehearsal dinner next Friday."

"Maybe we'll both have cooled down by then."

"Are you kidding? That old saying that absence makes the heart grow fonder goes double if you've had sex with that person."

"Sure, if it was good sex."

"Even if it wasn't. I almost went crazy in the days after that night together. I considered ambushing you in the school parking lot."

"You didn't hate me?"

"Hate you? I was obsessed with you. I wanted to try it again. I just knew it would be better."

"Anything would have been better." He hesitated. "Now that you mention it, I had the same thoughts."

"See? We didn't cool off. We wanted each other more."

"I wish you had ambushed me. I was so ashamed of myself I wasn't ever going to contact you, no matter how much I wanted to."

"And I thought you were so disappointed in me that you'd crossed me off your list."

"Ah, damn. I should have done something. Sent you flowers, or a nice card."

"A card? Do they make a card for that?"

"Okay, a blank card where I'd write… hell, I don't know. That I was sorry, that you're great but I'm a piece of garbage."

"I guess that would've helped."

"But I didn't do anything except leave you with hurt feelings. What a jerk."

"I got over it. Don't think you ruined my life or anything."

"Obviously I didn't. You got the degree you wanted and you went to Europe. I assume you like teaching at UM."

"Love it. I gave up on becoming a star and discovered that teaching potential stars is a blast."

"Sounds kind of like Mrs. Allred."

"Exactly. I'm glad she's still there. I don't always make it to the school musicals but I've managed to see about half of them."

"Me, too. I'm surprised we didn't run into each other."

"We almost did one year. I saw you and took off before you saw me."

"And that just sucks. Ten years of avoiding each other when if I'd just gotten over myself and reached out…"

"Don't beat yourself up. Even if you had contacted me, even if we'd had a summer romance, chances are it wouldn't have lasted beyond that."

"Maybe not, but you never—"

"Since the day I left for UM, my life's been in Missoula. I'm rarely in Wagon Train. I blocked out this week for the wedding, but when it's over,

I'm going back on Sunday. Got some prep work. I can't wait to dive in."

Her blunt assessment smarted, but it had the ring of truth. "I guess you don't come down much anymore." Could be that whenever he caught a glimpse of her, it made such an impression he imagined she was around more often than she actually was.

"When you're in theater, it's all-consuming. At least it is for me because I love it so much. Sometimes Mom and Dad will drive up and take me out to dinner because they haven't seen me in weeks."

"What about the five-year reunion? Did you have a conflict then?"

She hesitated. "Yes."

"A play?"

"No." She sighed. "You were the conflict."

"I'm sorry." He didn't know whether to feel bad about that or good because at least she wasn't indifferent to him. "Maybe I didn't ruin your life, but if fear of interacting with me made you skip the reunion, I—"

"It shouldn't have. I tried to psyche myself up to come. If I'd had a studly guy to bring, I might have toughed it out, but I didn't. For all I knew, you'd bring someone."

"Which I did."

"See? Like I said, you always had a girlfriend."

"Not that spring of the musical. Unless I can count you."

"Since you didn't take me to the prom, you can't count me."

"I almost asked you."

"You did? That's a shocker. Guess you changed your mind, then."

"Not until I overheard you tell someone you were going with Tony."

"Oh. Yeah, he really wanted to go but he needed a date who wouldn't expect it to be a romantic evening. You really would have asked me?"

"Yes, ma'am."

"You took somebody, though. Was it Geri?"

"We went as friends. Her fiancé was in the Army and couldn't get leave."

"In other words, you weren't dating anyone that spring, but you had your sights set on me?"

"You could say that."

"So hanging out with me on Senior Ditch Day wasn't exactly random, was it?"

"Not exactly."

"Just how premeditated was it?"

"I saw it as my last shot. When you suggested making it a twosome, I was overjoyed. Too bad I had to bring sex into the mix, though."

"The more we talk about it, the more I think we did the right thing."

"How do you figure *that*? It was a complete disaster."

"I used to believe it was, but after finding out you were a virgin, too, I see our mutual deflowering as sort of... sweet."

"You were sweet. I was pathetic." He pulled into the driveway of her parents' white two-story house, the nicest one on the block. Her father was the town doctor, after all, and her mother was an executive at the bank. He and Bret had worked with Liz Bradley to secure their business loan.

"Look at that." She turned to smile at him. "We talked the whole way back."

Her smile had been one of his favorite things about her, especially when it was directed at him. "Evidently we had a lot to say." He shut off the motor.

"I feel more comfortable with you, now."

"I guess I'm more comfortable with you, too." A relative term. Now that he wasn't driving, his skin tingled with the urge to make contact. "What now?"

"I've been thinking about that."

"Any ideas?"

"Since long talks make us more comfortable with each other, maybe we should hang out this week."

"On a friendship basis?" It was exactly what he should want. So why did it sound so depressing?

"Absolutely. We need to de-sensitize ourselves. If we get used to spending leisure time together, our interaction next weekend will come naturally because in a sense we'll spend the week rehearsing."

"Rehearsing." Only Faye would come up with something like that.

"Remember how nervous you were the first few rehearsals for *Grease*?"

"Yes, ma'am. I almost quit."

"But the more you did it, the easier it was, right?"

"It was, although the first night we had an audience, I got scared again, but once we got started, I was okay."

"This is the same idea. We'll practice being comfortable with each other this week."

"And by Friday afternoon we'll be besties?"

"Isn't that what we're going for? A risk-free, platonic relationship so we don't risk screwing up the family dynamic?"

"Well said." He'd processed very little of the conversation. His attention was elsewhere — on her musical voice, her quick breathing, the way her lips moved. His mouth was hungry for hers.

Could he spend more time with this beautiful woman and ignore his response? "I have a full work schedule this week."

"Then we'll have to get together in the evening."

"Guess so." Was she nuts? This plan was bound to fail and he was certifiable if he went along with it. Their chemistry was off the charts. Palling around this week would have a predictable, lusty result.

Giving in to that lust had the potential to create awkwardness or drama during the wedding festivities. That meant nixing her suggestion.

Unless....

Hm. Obviously she was immersed in her work, so dedicated that she rarely visited. Had she meant to emphasize how incompatible they were? In any case, message received. They had no future.

Was the answer to this issue lying there in plain sight? It wouldn't have worked ten years ago, but it might now that they were older, more experienced, more practical.

Faye shifted in her seat so she was facing him. "I don't know what you like to do for fun in the evenings."

He gave her a look.

"Besides that. You've made it clear that's a non-starter and I respect your decision. I'm sure we can come up with alternatives. How about catching a movie?"

"That's an idea."

"I'll check to see what's playing at the theater."

"We could also watch one at my place. Bigger selection."

"We could." There was a slight hesitation in her response.

"Too private?"

"I'll see what's playing at the Wheelhouse. I always loved that little theater even if it only has one screen."

Now that he had a possible solution, he might as well go along with her plan. "When do you want to go?"

"I'm free tomorrow night."

"I am, too. Come to think of it, I'm free all day. Want to go riding?"

She didn't answer right away and her expression was hard to read in the dim light. "You know what? That sounds nice. I miss riding out at the ranch. I haven't been since last summer with Marsh and Ella. Let's do that. Should I meet you at your cabin or the barn?"

"My cabin. Say around ten?"

"I'll be there."

"We'll put together a picnic lunch before we go." Sitting in a movie house that typically drew a decent crowd wasn't much of a test. A ride and a picnic would be.

Maybe they'd have a terrific time talking and admiring the scenery. He doubted it, but miracles did happen. If the outing went the way he pictured it, though, they'd struggle with overwhelming sexual tension. And now he had a Plan B to offer.

<u>6</u>

Faye drove her serviceable little sedan to Rowdy Ranch the next morning. She knew the way by heart, at least as far as the main house and the barn. Bypassing that turnoff, she kept an eye out for Gil's cabin. Would she recognize it in the daylight?

She should have asked Gil whether his road had some sort of landmark like a large rock or a fallen tree. But she'd been in a hurry to exit the truck when he'd brought her home. Although he'd opened his door, she'd put a stop to his obvious plan of walking her to the porch.

She'd been too vulnerable for that routine. He likely wouldn't have kissed her, but she might have kissed him. This morning she was jittery but resolved.

Gil's loyalty to his family impressed her and she would honor that. Sitting in a dark movie house watching something that might trigger the very emotions they were trying to avoid had been a bad suggestion. A ride in the fresh air was exactly the kind of wholesome activity to kick off this experiment.

But she should have insisted on meeting him at the barn instead. The GPS on her phone was no help. None of the cabins had addresses.

Was that it up ahead? She'd forgotten to look at the dashboard clock when she'd passed the turnoff to the main house so she had no clue how far she'd come.

The narrow road leading off to the right could be the one they'd headed down last night. Her pulse jittery, she took her foot off the gas so she could scan the area.

A structure partially obscured by trees was a McLintock cabin, but nothing about it looked familiar. Too many trees, for one thing. Hadn't the logs been stained a darker color?

She'd rather not pull up in front of the wrong place. Her trip out here wasn't a secret, but she didn't want to draw attention by arriving at a cabin that belonged to one of his siblings. She'd keep going.

On the seat beside her, her phone pinged. Putting on the brakes, she picked it up and read the text.

You just passed my road.

She sent him a thumbs-up emoji and turned around, heart thumping. She'd been on edge ever since waking up at dawn. Deep breathing exercises had helped but hadn't eliminated the familiar uneasiness in her stomach. Stage fright.

Made sense, in a way. She'd set this up as a rehearsal for next weekend and she had a role to play — Gil McLintock's platonic friend. It was the part he needed her to play and she'd give him the best performance she could manage.

If he'd seen her drive past his road, he must have been watching for her. Sure enough, he was waiting on the porch when she pulled in.

Since he wasn't wearing his hat, the sun highlighted streaks of red in his sandy hair. With his wide stance and his thumbs hooked in his belt loops, his hands framed the very part of him she should blur out. Two seconds into this plan and she was already in trouble.

Did cowboys stand that way on purpose? She'd never asked and she wouldn't be asking this morning. Her male colleagues in the theater department sometimes wore jeans, but the effect was totally different, maybe because they didn't pair the jeans with boots and a yoked shirt.

None of them had the muscle definition to fill out that shirt like Gil did, either. Ten years of working with a hammer and forge looked good on him. Real good. She might have overestimated her ability to resist—

He raised his hand, palm out like a traffic cop.

She hit the brakes as heat rose to her cheeks. She'd almost smacked into his porch. Taking a quick breath, she rolled down her window as he descended the steps. "Where should I park?"

He grinned. "You can leave it right here if you want. Saves you some steps."

"I'm not leaving it here. I got distracted by... something on the radio."

His grin widened. "I don't hear a radio."

"That's because — oh, never mind. How about over by your truck?"

"That'll do." Laughter sparkled in his blue eyes.

"Having fun?"

"Yes, ma'am."

She put the car in reverse, backed up and drove over to the spot where his truck sat gleaming in the sunlight. Not a speck of mud on it and yet after driving on muddy roads the night before, it should have been splattered with the stuff.

She tucked her wallet and keys under the seat even though she probably could have left both in plain sight. She was on Rowdy Ranch property.

The McLintocks dazzled her. Always had. When she was a kid, she'd envied Ella's close friendship with Marsh and had been grateful they'd let her tag along most of the time.

Those two had bonded the day they'd met in kindergarten. She and Gil had not. Theirs was a more complicated relationship, one that required careful navigation.

Showtime. Grabbing her phone and hat, she climbed out and walked over to where he stood waiting. "Did you wash your truck?"

"I did."

"Nice job, but are you a magician?"

"Why?"

"I don't know how you washed it without creating puddles and more mud."

"I took it over to Mom's. She has the setup — a cement pad with a water line and hose bib. We're all welcome to use it in exchange for keeping her truck looking spotless."

"So that's why hers is never dirty. I used to marvel at that."

"In the beginning it was kind of a pain for Sky, or so he claims, since he was the only kid with a truck he liked keeping clean. When Beau bought one, they shared the job of washing Mom's, so that helped. It's more fun if there's two of us. This morning Rance and I were truck-washing buddies."

"You must have been up early, then."

"Always am. Ready to go make some sandwiches?"

"Sure." She fell into step beside him. "How come you don't have a walkway up to your steps?"

"I like to leave it clear so pretty ladies can drive right up to my porch."

"Can we just forget I did that?"

"I don't think so. Some moments stick with you forever."

"It was your fault."

"Oh?"

"I told myself I wouldn't ask this, but now that I can see you won't let it go, I've changed my mind. I was distracted by the way you were standing there."

"That's how I always stand. Nothing unusual about it."

"With your feet apart and your thumbs hooked in your belt loops?"

"Yep. That about describes my pattern."

"Is it a cowboy thing?"

"I hadn't thought about that, but I suppose so. Why?"

"Because when you do that, your hands just naturally showcase your privates. Is that on purpose?"

He cracked up. "That's what you were thinking about when you almost drove up on my porch?"

"Yes, dammit! I'm anticipating a day filled with wholesome activities that have nothing to do with sex. Then I pull into your front yard and—"

"There I am!" Still laughing, he jogged up the steps. "A billboard for gettin' it on."

"You haven't answered my question." She followed him across the porch. "Is it on purpose?"

Opening the door, he held it for her. "No, ma'am." He cleared the laughter from his throat. "At least not intentionally on my part. Want me to check with my brothers and get back to you with their answers?"

"No! You're not allowed to tell your brothers I asked about this. Ever."

"Then it'll be our little secret."

"Yes, please." She stepped into his living room. It had looked inviting last night with only a single lamp on. This morning, with sunlight spilling through the windows, details emerged that she'd missed before.

The roomy sofa sitting in front of the fireplace with overstuffed armchairs on either side formed a cozy half-circle. To her right, a round table and four chairs created an intimate dining area. A chandelier of intricate ironwork hung above the table.

She pointed to it. "Did you make that?"

"Joint venture. Bret and I worked on it together."

"It's lovely. Are you selling those, now?"

"We just started. Looks like it'll be a popular item. Come on in the kitchen. If we stand here talking all day we'll never get sandwiches made."

"You don't have to twist my arm to get me into your amazing kitchen."

He gestured her toward it and she let out a little happy sigh as she walked through the arched doorway. "It's even prettier in the morning."

"That's the sign of a good kitchen." He opened the fridge and started pulling things out. "Bread's in the breadbox if you want to get it."

"I never would have guessed." She took a fragrant loaf out of a curved blue container with BREAD labeled on the outside. "What me to slice it?"

"Go right ahead. Cutting board's hanging up on the—"

"Found it." She took a large knife from a sturdy block and got to work. "And you're both still shoeing horses?"

"We are." He brought the sandwich fixings over to the counter, took down a second cutting board and began assembling sandwiches from the bread she cut. "We have more work than we can handle, especially this time of year. We've been working Saturdays lately, but not next Saturday, obviously."

"I can tell you enjoy it." She stopped slicing.

"I do, especially since we expanded into the metalworks concept. The business has turned out way better than Bret and I imagined, and we had big dreams as kids."

"I'm happy for you."

"I'm happy for us, too. Sandwich bags are in the drawer right beside you if you'd like to package these up."

"I'm on it. You know, talking about this reminds me of something. Did you have a reason to drive into town last night, like you told my dad?"

"I made that up."

"I knew it. Did you make up the other part, too? That you had something that belongs to me?"

"No. That's true." He handed her the last sandwich and started chopping up a couple of carrots.

"Okay, then. Enough mystery. I want to see it." She tucked the sandwich in the bag.

"What's wrong with a little mystery?" He grabbed a sandwich bag and dumped in the carrot pieces.

"A little mystery is fine. A lot of mystery gets annoying. This one has dragged on long enough, especially when I'm convinced it'll turn out to be something lame that you came up with on the fly."

"Would I do such a thing?" After rinsing and drying the boards, he hung them up again.

"Oh, yes."

"Well, from my perspective, I don't think it's been dragged out nearly long enough." He took a satchel from a bottom cupboard and loaded the sandwiches into it along with the bag of carrot chunks and a couple of cloth napkins. "But since you're clearly agitated about it, I promise to produce this valuable item once we get to our picnic spot. It'll give us something to talk about."

"Like we have that problem."

"I guess that's what happens when you have a ten-year backlog of topics to cover."

"How big is this item?"

"Not telling you." He picked up the satchel and a thermos that was sitting on the counter.

"Must not be very big if you're planning to smuggle it out of here and take it on the ride without me knowing."

"I'll neither confirm nor deny. There's two tin cups in the cupboard by your shoulder. Would you get them, please?"

She found the cups. "Is this thing you have fragile? I'd hate to have it break while you're transporting it."

"Not fragile." He opened the satchel. "Just tuck the cups along the side and the sandwiches won't get squished."

"I'm dying of curiosity."

He smiled. "Let's go."

He had the instincts of an actor, a trait that got her every time. He had her in the palm of his hand.

7

Over the years, Gil had taken several of his dates horseback riding. Usually that put him in the role of mentor as they tacked up the horses and started out on the trail. Not so with Faye.

She was an old hand at this, even knew which horse she'd like to ride. On the way to the barn, she'd texted Marsh and asked for permission to take out Pie and borrow Marsh's saddle. The future bridegroom had thanked her for giving his horse some attention since he'd been tied up with wedding stuff recently.

Once they'd arrived, Faye settled right into the routine, even offering to put a saddlebag on Pie and carry their lunch. He'd tied a rolled picnic blanket behind his saddle and they'd hit the trail in record time. Just like with the sandwich-making, they worked efficiently together. Twenty-four hours ago he wouldn't have guessed that was possible.

His worries that he'd want to grab her the minute she came within range hadn't been a problem. She'd kept him too busy. Teasing her about the item currently resting in the pocket of his jeans had been the closest he'd come to flirting.

She hadn't flirted with him at all. Instead, she'd dived right into forbidden territory on arrival with her comment about his hands framing his junk. Sassy woman.

That sass had charmed him ten years ago and had led him to believe she had more knowledge about sex than he'd had. Ironically, she'd assumed the same about him.

That said, hooking his thumbs in his belt loops was *not* something he did to signal his junk was poised for action. Or was it?

The issue ricocheted around in his brain as they meandered down the shady trail through a stand of pine and aspen, Faye and Pie in the lead.

He wouldn't repeat the conversation to his brothers. He'd promised her not to. But he could take a poll without revealing why he was asking. He could say he read it somewhere, or heard it on—

"This feels so good."

Her comment ended his noodling on sexual signaling and landed him smack-dab in a puddle of lust. It wasn't just the words. It was the way she said them, her voice rich with appreciation. "Glad you like it."

"I used to crave taking this path at a trot and then racing across the meadow, but there's something to be said for moseying along listening to the birds and the clip-clop of hooves."

"And enjoying the view." Vegetation had narrowed the trail to a one-lane and following her gave him the freedom to admire her tempting fanny without getting in trouble for it.

"I know, right? At least a dozen shades of green, flowers still blooming in the woods, and a glimpse of the Sapphires through breaks in the trees. I really don't get outside enough. Thanks for suggesting this."

"You're more than welcome."

"Fall is in the air. I can feel it. How about you?"

"Yes, ma'am." He was feeling it, all right. The tingle running though his body might be due to the approach of fall. But he'd bet the woman riding ahead of him was generating the electricity.

"Wouldn't it be awesome if the northern lights showed up during the wedding reception?"

"Sure would. We're late enough in the month that it's possible. We've seen them in August before."

"Ella really wants that to happen. She would have a better chance in September, but since we're both teachers... not doable."

"Is she checking the aurora forecast?" The northern lights were one of his favorite subjects.

"Oh, yeah. She's keeping track of the K-index. Did you know the lights peak every eleven years?"

"I did. Happened our senior year, which means we have another one coming up in the next twelve months or so."

"If it was my wedding, I'd probably postpone it until spring break and try to catch that show."

"You couldn't have the wedding outside, though. You'd freeze your ass off."

"Sure you could. You could build a huge bonfire and the ceremony would be in front of it, with guests clustered around, all bundled up. The ceremony would have to be short because you don't want to stand still too long, but that would be fine with me. I like a short ceremony, personally."

"Me, too. Short and to the point."

"Then after the ceremony, you serve hot toddies, blast music through some speakers and dance to keep warm."

"Aren't you supposed to eat after the wedding?" Although her plan sounded terrific. Low stress with the potential for a light show overhead.

"Eating afterward is traditional, but why not have the feast before the wedding? Everybody can socialize, have a few drinks, eat good food, loosen up. The ceremony would be way more fun."

"Sounds good to me. I'm always starving by the time the bride and groom arrive for the reception."

"Partly because of the picture thing. I say do that mid-afternoon."

"But there's that superstition about the groom not seeing the bride that day until she walks down the aisle."

"I know, and it's all very dramatic. But if I could have a ceremony in front of a bonfire with northern lights streaming through the sky, I'd ditch that center-aisle entrance in a heartbeat."

"Yeah, me, too." He could see her putting that plan into action when she found Mr. Right. "I might steal that idea." If he could find someone who would go along with it.

"Be my guest. It's not copyrighted." She swiveled around to glance at him. "You probably don't remember that Ella and I made some nighttime trips out to the ranch that winter because the lights are more spectacular out here. Marsh invited us. My folks came one time, too."

"Now that you mention it, I do remember. I hope I didn't do or say anything stupid. I was pretty full of myself."

"Yes, you were."

He made a face. "Appreciate the honesty."

"That's me. I tell it like it is." She gave him a cute little smile and faced forward again.

"In that case, since I was clearly a pain in the ass, what did you think when I got the part of Danny?"

"Well…"

"Don't worry about hurting my feelings."

"I figured you'd be more exciting to kiss than Tony."

"That's it? Come on. I had no experience. You had to wonder if I'd ruin the production."

"Okay, I did wonder if Mrs. Allred had made a terrible mistake."

"Aha! So you didn't want me there."

"I didn't say that. I wanted you there."

"Why?"

"Because you were incredibly good looking and even if the musical turned into a disaster I didn't care because I'd get to spend a lot of time with you and be required to kiss you. I was in heaven."

His chest tightened. She'd had a huge crush on him. Then he'd taken her virginity and… in her view… dumped her. She'd been in heaven and he'd left her in hell. "Faye, I'm so sorry."

She turned back to him again. "I'm not trying to lay a guilt trip on you. You asked for the truth and that's it, but as I've said before, I got over it. I moved on."

"I'm glad." And she'd just burned Plan B to the ground.

*<u>**8**</u>*

Faye recognized the small clearing where Gil suggested they stop to eat lunch. The ranch had several lovely spots, but she especially liked this one. On the far side stood a giant ponderosa, its trunk a good three feet in diameter with branches reaching more than a hundred feet into the blue sky.

As they rode in, she pointed to it. "I've always loved that big ol' tree. I'm glad you brought us here."

"You must have come to this meadow with Ella and Marsh."

"Yep, when we were kids. We'd spread our blanket under that tree. It's even bigger, now."

"Which means more shade so we won't roast. Fall may be in the air but it's still summer on the ground."

"When you're right, you're right." She dismounted and dropped Pie's reins to the grass. The gelding, who was named after Jimmy Stewart's favorite horse, would stay put. Gil did the same with Dollar, who was named after John Wayne's favorite horse.

After she pulled out the satchel and retrieved the bag of carrot pieces, she and Gil fed the horses their reward. Pie's mouth tickled her palm as he carefully scooped up the treat. "They're such good horses."

"The best."

"Do you think they're movie star material like their namesakes?"

"I'm sure they could be, but nobody has enough money to take this horse from me and Marsh would say the same."

"I'm sure he would."

"How come you got the one named for John Wayne's horse? That seems super special."

"Luck of the draw. "He's the look-alike Mom happened to find when I turned fourteen. We drove to Boise to get him."

"I was pea-green with envy that each of you got horses when you were fourteen. I thought you were all the luckiest duckies in the world."

"Did you ever get one?"

"Oh, I tried. I was twelve when Marsh got Pie. He let Ella and me ride him a little, like around the corral. That's when I started saving. I was determined I'd have one when I turned fourteen."

"And your folks said no?"

"That's right."

"I doubt you took that lying down."

"No, sir. I was relentless. Finally Mom took me aside. They'd help me get a horse, but I'd have to give up my plan to study theater at UM. Instead I'd need to stay here and find a job that allowed me to see my horse every day because I would be his or her best friend by then."

"Smart lady."

"When I saw it from the horse's perspective, I had to give up my plan, but I decided once I became a movie star, I'd buy a ranch and have a whole herd of horses so they wouldn't miss me when I was working on a film."

"I'm a little surprised you didn't make that happen."

"Be serious, Gil." She looked him in the eye. "Can you see me as a movie star?"

"Yes."

Her heart quivered. One word, and he'd paid her an extravagant compliment she'd remember for a very long time. She could kiss him. But that would start something. She wasn't here to start something. "Thank you."

"I believe you can do anything you set your mind to and it sounds like you really wanted that herd of horses."

Oh, how she cherished the note of respect in his voice. "In a way, I have one. I make a monthly donation to an organization that protects wild mustangs and burros."

The warmth of his smile wrapped around her like a hug. "Perfect."

Now she *really* wanted to kiss him. She needed to give her mouth something else to do. "Let's eat."

He held her gaze a moment longer, then nodded. "You bet. I'll go spread out the quilt if you'll bring over the food and the thermos."

"Will do." And she'd take enough time to let her kissing urge fade. Hoisting their lunch over her shoulder, she dug out the thermos. Then she gave Pie a scratch under his silky mane. "Thanks for bringing me out here, buddy."

The gelding curved his neck in her direction and rubbed his nose against her arm. She stroked the star-shaped blaze on his forehead. "Be back soon." Yeah, the monthly donation fit her circumstances, but it didn't quite do the trick.

She gave Pie a kiss on the nose before starting over toward the big ponderosa. Friendly and platonic. She could do this.

Or not. Lordy, that cowboy stirred her up.

On his hands and knees, Gil smoothed the wrinkles out of the multicolored patchwork quilt. She'd provided enough time for him to take off his boots, which sat beside him on the grass. He'd propped his hat on top.

He'd also rolled back his sleeves. Shouldn't be a big deal. It wasn't like he'd taken off his shirt. But she wanted him to.

The supple grace of his muscled forearms gave her a tempting preview of what promised to be a spectacular show. Sunlight muted by feathery pine needles created a soft-focus scene right out of a romantic movie.

An R-rated one, too. She wanted to roll around on that quilt with the guy in the starring role.

Lifting his head, he sat back on his heels. "Something wrong?"

"No." She scrambled for an excuse. "I was just thinking… that looks too nice for a picnic. What if we get food on it?"

He shrugged. "It's happened before. It washes. If a stain doesn't come out, it's so colorful you don't even notice. Makes a good tablecloth."

"Alrighty then." Taking a deep breath, she let it out slowly as she walked toward him, conscious of his steady blue gaze. Could he tell she was hyperventilating? That she was fighting a sensual pull that might be stronger than her self-control?

He'd called the quilt a tablecloth. That helped. She'd never had sex on a tablecloth, which by definition covered a table. Never had sex on one of those, either, maybe because she'd lacked sufficient inspiration.

She had it now, in spades. What he called a tablecloth she called a convenient soft surface for two people to stretch out and have some fun.

He'd look good naked. All the evidence pointed to it — the snug fit of his shirt, the light dusting of hair on his forearms, the way his thighs stretched the faded denim of his jeans.

"I recommend taking off your boots."

Okay, so she'd been standing and staring for... no telling how long. "That was my plan. Let me give you these." She handed over the satchel and thermos before turning her back, sitting down and pulling off her boots.

Not looking at him should have eased the tension. But she could still smell his aftershave and hear him breathing.

"Plain socks, I see."

"Absolutely. No stage fright here." Yeah, that had evaporated ages ago.

"Are you sure you're okay?"

"I'm fine." Taking a page out of his book, she laid her hat on top of her boots, pushed herself to her feet and turned around.

Oh, boy. The satchel lay unopened. He hadn't changed position, either. Evidently he'd spent the whole time sitting on his heels watching her pull off her boots.

Judging from the way he was looking at her, he was thinking what she was thinking. If she gave in, he might, too, against his better judgment. And hers. That was a sure-fire way to end up with a wagonload of regrets.

She'd better do something, and fast. Another mention of food might not be compelling enough to drag them away from the cliff. They needed something more dramatic. But she was totally out of—

"Come on down here." He held her gaze as he patted the space across from him.

Her breath hitched. "Okay." If he broke first, odds were good she'd fold immediately. Heart racing, she stepped onto the blanket and sat cross-legged facing him.

Rising to his knees, he pulled something out of his pocket.

"You're finally giving me the thing you found from the musical?" Brilliant move. She'd forgotten all about it. Luckily he hadn't.

"Seems like I should. We're here." He shifted into a cross-legged position, mirroring her.

"I agree. Excellent timing." Relief left her breathless. "I thought you'd hand me the program." She looked at his closed fist. "But it can't be unless you've turned it into a Shrinky Dink."

"That would make no sense."

"A lot of things I turned into a Shrinky Dink made no sense but I loved the process so much I kept making stuff. And by the way, I have a program."

"You didn't shred it after the way I treated you?"

"That would have been stupid. I got the whole cast to sign it. I would never destroy it. I just took a felt-tipped pen to your signature."

"Oh." His mouth tilted up at the corners. "Well done. Exactly what I deserved."

"Now I wish I hadn't."

"I could always sign it again."

"Hey, there's an idea. I just might have you do that." Good. Conversation was flowing. They'd disconnected the wire on the ticking time bomb. "Clearly this thing is small enough to fit in your hand."

"Yes, ma'am."

"Is it a wadded-up hair bow?"

"Nope."

"Oh, wait, I know. It's memories. You'll open your hand and nothing's there, but you're ready to spout off a bunch of memories whenever I want to hear them."

"Interesting idea. Would you like that?"

"Probably. Did I guess it?"

"No, you did not. I'll give you a hint. It's a prop."

"A prop? I can't imagine a prop that small."

"Can't you?" He held her gaze.

"Oh." She gulped. Not something silly. Not at all.

<u>9</u>

Gil opened his hand. His high school class ring lay in his palm. He'd been right about where he'd stowed it — in a velvet box in the far corner of his underwear drawer. He'd polished it up last night after he'd come home from dropping Faye off at her folks' house.

Wearing a ring when shoeing horses was dangerous. You could lose a finger. Despite having settled on that profession by his senior year, he'd bought one anyway as a keepsake.

Turned out he'd needed it as a prop for the moment in *Grease* when Danny gives Sandy his class ring. Mrs. Allred could have found a cheesy fake one, but he'd volunteered his.

Faye had given it back after the last performance and he'd kept it in that velvet box ever since. When he'd come up with his story the night before, he'd decided the ring might work. Technically it wasn't hers, but it could be. A souvenir from the musical, right? Why not?

"Gil, I can't take that."

"Can't or won't?

"Can't. You paid the money, and they weren't cheap, which is why I didn't get one. My mom even offered to pay, but they were already helping out with my UM tuition so I said no."

"All the more reason to take mine, which is going to waste in my dresser drawer."

"Except it's yours. Even has your birthstone."

He smiled. "You remember our birthday thing?"

"I'm a walking database of birthdays. I can't seem to help myself."

"Especially when yours is the day after mine."

"Probably has something to do with it." Then her eyes widened. "Oh, my God." Then she started to laugh.

"What?"

"We're both *Virgos*. Sign of the Virgin. I guess that night down by the creek was written in the stars."

He grinned. "Maybe." He was beginning to wonder if it had been. "In any case, a sapphire's your birthstone, too."

"That's still not enough reason to give me your class ring." She swallowed a gulp of laughter. "Unless you want to go steady."

He snorted because that was the right response. And ignored the tug on his heart. "Any minute now we'll bust out with *Summer Nights*."

"You first."

"I'll pass. But you go right ahead."

"I'm not doing it by myself. Do you sing these days?"

"Sometimes." He'd admit to that much, but he'd rather not reveal the extent of his continued love for that musical. Or singing and dancing in general. If Bret caught wind of it, he could take it the wrong way.

"You should keep it up so you don't get rusty."

"That reminds me. At the five-year reunion we had quite a few liquored-up cast members ready to perform *Summer Nights*. I told them I couldn't do it without you."

"That was sweet."

"No, that was my excuse. They tried to get Leslie to take your part."

"Oh, no." Faye clapped a hand to her mouth. "Whoops. That wasn't nice."

"But true. I was terrified she'd agree. It wouldn't have been pretty."

"What if I had been there? Would you have chickened out?"

"Oh, I probably would have done it. Right after I had another beer." He paused. "You should come this year."

"Do you care if they ask us to sing?"

"Nah. I'll practice."

"Oh, you know what? I could help you this week! I'll be your coach!"

"Uh...no." She'd quickly find out he didn't need practice.

"Why not? It's just me. We could start right now. It'll be like old times."

He soaked up the sparkle in those gray eyes. Could he pretend? Sing off-key on purpose? Probably not.

"Look, I understand if you're self-conscious, but I really could help."

"Let me think about it." He picked up the ring and the sapphire flashed in the sunlight. Maybe giving it to her was a dopey idea. "If you really don't want this, you don't have to—"

"I didn't say that. It's gorgeous. I don't know if the sapphire's real or synthetic, but it's very pretty. Matches your John Travolta eyes." She batted her lashes at him.

"Here we go." She'd come up with the *John Travolta eyes* label during their first rehearsal and everyone had riffed on it for the duration. "You'll be happy to know our former cast members ran that one into the ground at the reunion."

"Awesome. Now I'm really sorry I wasn't there."

"As to the street value of this sapphire, it's synthetic. I wanted a keepsake, not an heirloom."

"See? You wanted a *keep*sake. Which means you need to *keep* it."

"Very funny. I should have ordered a beer mug instead. I can't wear this and it's not like I'm going to display it somewhere."

"And you think I'd wear it? Wrap tape around it so it would fit?"

He rolled his eyes. "*No.* That's not where I was going with this. Theater became your career. I thought you might like a prop from that musical. Who knows? You might decide to have your UM students put on *Grease* and you could use it again."

"Interesting you should say that. One of the kids mentioned recently that it would be a cool project."

"And you said?"

"That I'd seriously consider it. The guy who suggested it has the chops to pull off Danny."

"Then clearly you need this. It doesn't require much storage room. I'll give you the box when we get back." The longer he talked about it, the more convinced he was that the ring belonged with her.

"If I agree, will you promise to stop feeling guilty about taking my virginity?"

He jerked back. "What? That has nothing to do with why I—"

"Gil." Her voice gentled. "You know it does. Rings are highly symbolic. And by the way, feeling guilty about it is dumb because I took your virginity, too."

"It's not the same."

"It is the same except I didn't know you were a virgin until you told me last night. I suppose I should have guessed since you had no staying power, but I blamed the booze."

"Would you have felt guilty if I'd told you that night?"

Her brow crinkled the way it used to when she was trying to remember a line. Then the slight furrow disappeared. "No, I wouldn't."

"Why not?"

"For the same reason you shouldn't. We both wanted to do it. And you had no idea I was a first-timer."

He sighed. "All right. Point taken. Two drunk virgins have no business having sex. There was bad judgment on both sides."

"Agreed. So now you can—"

"But I blew the follow-up." He dropped the ring back into his palm. "This doesn't fix anything, but I hope it'll remind you that I'm very sorry for being the jerk who didn't reach out afterward. I should have."

She studied it, her forehead crinkling again. Then she looked up. "In the interest of easing your conscience, I'll take it."

"Okay, but I also hoped that giving it to you would...." He trailed off, out of words.

"Help me forgive you? Because I already have. I don't need the ring for that."

"Not forgive, exactly, just—"

"Think kindly of you whenever I look at it?"

"Yes. That's what I'm after. I want to be a good memory, not a bad one."

"You will be." She picked it up, her fingers brushing the palm of his hand. Leaning back, she managed to shove it deep into the front pocket of her jeans. "Thank you."

So that was that. Moving on. Except when the discussion had circled back to the miserable sex they'd had years ago, he'd hopped back on the temptation train.

He couldn't ask for a better outcome for this picnic than having her accept the ring as a gesture of friendship. Mission accomplished. But his ego was back in charge, whispering in his ear.

If they'd come this far, why not go a step farther and show her how much he'd learned since that awful first encounter? By pleasing her while taking nothing for himself, he could erase any lingering memory of his clumsy performance.

He told his ego to take a hike and opened the satchel. "Ready to eat?"

"Uh-huh. I'm starving."

"Me, too." He hadn't gone into acting after high school, but he'd learned that he had a flair for it. That talent would come in handy this week.

<u>10</u>

The circular imprint of Gil's class ring pressing against Faye's thigh created a seductive bond, but where else was she supposed to put it? Inside her bra?

Taking it might have been a mistake, but there was no turning back, now. Yeah, she'd wanted it. His grand gesture of using it in the musical had thrilled her eighteen-year-old heart.

He'd asked her to take charge of it until the final performance so it wouldn't get lost. While she'd scoffed at the outdated tradition of wearing a guy's class ring on a chain, she'd secretly loved having temporary possession of one with Gil's name on it.

Now it was hers for good, and he obviously wanted her to have it. She'd treasure it more than he would ever know.

"I hope you can manage without a plate." He opened the satchel and gave her a forest-green napkin.

"Sure can." Shaking it out, she spread it on her lap. The satchel sat between them, but their knees nearly touched. The scent of sun-warmed denim blended with the aroma of fresh bread and the tang of mustard. His bronzed forearms flexed as he dug out the sandwiches and handed her one.

"Thanks." She took half the sandwich out of the bag. "You've been outside a lot."

"As much as possible." He laid his sandwich in his lap and reached for the thermos. "Shoeing horses is way more fun for me in the summer."

"I'll bet." Fun to watch, too. She ran the video in her head — Gil in a sleeveless T-shirt, a horse's hind leg tucked between his knees, a hammer in his hand, a sheen of sweat on his biceps... *down, girl.*

She breathed in, let the air out slowly and turned the dial from sizzle to serene. "This brings back many good memories. Thanks for suggesting we come out here."

"I hope those memories include lemonade." He handed her a brimming cup.

"They sure do. We used to make our own sandwiches, but Marybeth always supplied the fresh lemonade." She took a sip. "Tastes just like I remember. Did she make it?"

"Nope. I did." He poured his lemonade. "Marybeth taught us how. According to her, she worked herself out of a job she loved doing."

"Well, here's to Marybeth." She touched her cup to his.

"To Marybeth." He took a long swallow.

His throat was sun-kissed where he'd left the top two buttons of his shirt undone. She longed to put aside her lunch and nuzzle him there. His warm skin would taste salty....

"Marybeth's a gem. Buck, too."

"Yep, they're great." Had he caught her ogling?

Evidently not. He was happily munching on his sandwich, his gaze mellow. He chewed and swallowed. "I don't know how Mom would've managed if they hadn't come along."

"How did she find them?" She bit into her sandwich, which was delicious, but not the taste she craved.

"The story goes that they found her. She was in grocery shopping hell with Sky trying to climb out of the cart and Beau screeching like a banshee. Marybeth and Buck came to her rescue, and she offered them a job."

"And now they don't exactly have one?"

"They do, but it's not as intense. Mom loves having Marybeth handle most of the cooking, and although Sky's officially in charge of the barn, he'd be stretched thin without Buck. Then there's Maverick and Zach to fuss over. Babies are back in the mix."

"And two more on the way." She polished off half her sandwich and pulled out the other half.

"The grandkids can't come fast enough for Marybeth and Buck. Or Mom. The ranch was set up for babies from the get-go."

"Do they have names, yet?"

"I asked last night. Still up in the air." He started eating the rest of his sandwich.

"I couldn't stand that uncertainty." She took another bite.

"Me, either. I'd have settled that long ago."

"Absolutely." Not looking at him while they talked would be rude. But every glance increased her obsession with his mouth—the supple movement of his lips, the sensual flick of his tongue swiping away a drop of mustard.

Glancing down, she finished her sandwich. She was losing this battle with herself. She'd never been so desperate to kiss a man.

A very silent man. For some reason he'd stopped talking. When she lifted her head, her gaze collided with his. What she saw in those blue eyes stole her breath.

He swallowed. "Faye, I—" His chest heaved and he glanced away.

"What?"

"Nothing." He reached for the satchel. "We have another sandwich. Would you—"

"Were you thinking what I thought you were?"

"Probably." He made eye contact again. "It would be a mistake."

"So you've said."

"Nothing's changed. I just keep remembering that night. It had promise but we missed out."

"I think about it, too, but—"

"You need someone from up there, someone who's a better fit."

She nodded. If only she could forget that glorious moment when *he'd* been a perfect fit. So far she'd failed spectacularly.

"I hope you find him."

"I hope so, too." And she would continue the search after she left town next Sunday night. But in the meantime, she had a problem in need of a solution. Then it came to her, jolting her heart into a frenzied rhythm and sending a trickle of sweat down her spine. "One thing's for sure. I won't find him this week."

"True. You'll be busy helping Ella with her wedding."

She sucked in air and took the plunge. "I also need to diffuse whatever this is between us. I'm struggling. So are you."

His breath hitched. "Yes, ma'am."

"Look, we're not eighteen anymore. What if we just—"

"No. You had a huge crush on me. I broke your heart. I can't take a chance on—"

"You won't be taking the chance. I will."

Clearly that knocked him back a little. "I suppose, but—"

She had the bit in her teeth, now. She was going for it. "It's gallant of you to worry about hurting me, but... it's a wee bit condescending."

"It is?"

"You're trying to protect me as if I'm that dreamy-eyed girl you used to know."

"I'm only—"

"I get it. You've carried that image around for ten years. But I'm a grown woman with enough sexual experience to visualize what having sex with you would be like. If we don't get it on, I'll be a hot mess by next weekend."

He gulped. "Message received."

"The way I see it, there are only two ways this can go wrong in a way that could affect our families or the wedding — I let you break my heart, or you let me break yours."

He held her gaze for a long moment. "Nicely put."

Her skin flushed. Victory was at hand. "I can handle a week of sexy times with you just fine, Gil McLintock. What do you say? Are you in?"

Heat flared in his blue eyes. He dragged in a breath. "Yes, ma'am."

She quivered as adrenaline shot through her. No guts, no glory. "Let's do this."

<u>11</u>

Gil had never tried cliff-diving, but it probably felt like this. You had to just throw yourself over the edge and pray you hadn't made a fatal decision.

He briefly considered tackling her right where she sat, but that lacked class. Setting aside the satchel, he stood and held out his hand. Managed to keep it from shaking as he looked into luminous gray eyes that had haunted him for years. "You honor me, Faye."

Her breath caught and her cheeks turned pink as she put her hand in his. "What a lovely thing to say."

"I mean it." He drew her to her feet and into his arms. He hadn't meant to groan when he pulled her close, but damn. She'd been on the skinny side the last time he'd held her. "You feel so good."

"You, too." Nestling against him, she threaded her fingers through his hair as she cupped the back of his head. "You're so...solid."

He smiled. "Some parts more than others."

"You weren't expecting this."

"I was not."

"Should we pack up and ride back to your cabin?"

"Not yet."

Her color deepened. "Oh. I guess that would be painful for you."

"That's not my reason. First things first." His attention drifted to her mouth. "I'd given up hope of ever doing this again." He slowly lowered his head, absorbing everything — the flutter of her lashes, her breathing going shallow, her chin lifting, her lips parting in a silent invitation. *For him.*

A rush of emotion tightened his chest. Kissing Faye had been a privilege he'd been given ten years ago. He'd squandered it. Not this time.

When he touched down, her little gasp grabbed him by the heart, the one he wouldn't let her break. He might have lied about that.

The velvet texture of her lips tore another groan from his chest. Fighting the urge to lay claim, he brushed his mouth over hers, ran his tongue lightly over her cupid's bow and her plump lower lip.

Her fingers tightened against his scalp. "More."

That whispered plea chipped away a layer of his control, but he was determined to set down easy, take his time, make slight adjustments until he found... there, right there.

Ten years evaporated. When his lips melded with hers and his tongue began to explore the richness of her mouth, recognition surged through him, leaving him dizzy with gratitude.

Moaning, he took the kiss deeper, tunneling his fingers through her hair, tilting her head and changing position. The ravaging had begun. He'd crossed the line from polite to primal, coaxing her into the realm of total surrender.

And she gave it, slackening her jaw, molding her body to his, immersing him in a rippling flood of sensation. Had he made the right decision to jump off that cliff? Hell, yeah.

His chest strained at the buttons of his shirt. Her nimble fingers freed them one by one and stroked the territory she uncovered, flattening her palms against his rapidly beating heart.

She'd only touched him like this once, but his skin remembered the sensation, yearned for more. Wrenching her T-shirt from the waistband of her jeans, he broke the kiss long enough to pull it over her head and toss it away. Her bra followed.

She hummed as he gathered her close. Shuddering with pleasure when the satin warmth of her breasts made contact, he returned to the joy of tasting her sweet mouth. If he could only have this, he'd die a happy man.

But she deserved more. Her curvy bottom fit nicely into his cupped hands as he lifted her off her feet. Clearly she knew her part. Wrapping her arms around his shoulders and her legs around his hips, she tightened her grip as he knelt on the quilt and lowered her to the fluffy surface.

She'd entered into the dance of tongues, stroking hers along the length of his. She was experienced all right and he could read her mind. What she was silently proposing might happen in the future, but not in this meadow. He had a debt to pay and it had come due.

He played the game with her, thrilling to her feisty assertiveness while he worked her out of her jeans and satisfyingly damp panties. What he had in mind shouldn't take much time, which meant he could tack on another one.

Was he in pain? Oh, yeah. But he could wait. They had hours ahead of them and he planned to make every minute count.

He eased away from the kiss gradually, moving to her cheeks, her chin, the hollow of her throat, pressing his mouth against her racing pulse.

"I know—" She paused to gulp for air. "I know what you're up to."

"Do you, now?" He dropped light kisses on the curve of her breast. "Any objections?"

Her laughter was almost a hiccup. "No objections if you'll let me—"

"We'll talk." He circled her rosy nipple with his tongue. Now he knew the color. Ten years ago the woods had been dark and their lovemaking, if it could be called that, had provided only shades of gray.

This was better. He kissed a small mole on her other breast. He could spend all day here fondling the womanly shape of her, but he had important business elsewhere. Sliding lower, he nipped and licked his way to operation central, hidden by soft brown curls.

By the time he planted kisses on her inner thigh, she was trembling.

"You're a bold one, cowboy."

"I have my priorities." Sliding his hands under her hips, he leaned in and flicked his tongue right where it would have the most impact.

She cried out.

"I'll take that as a yes."

"Yes."

"Then here we go." Closing his eyes, he settled in, heart thumping, cock straining and her whimpers music to his ears. She was drenched. He feasted on the nectar of her desire, gloried in her willingness to open to him, to be vulnerable, to let him give her what he so needed to bestow.

When she arched upward and filled the meadow with joyous sounds of release, he was jubilant. Good thing those horses were steady.

Tuning into her quivering body, he caught her on the downslope of her orgasm and coaxed her back up. She came a second time, gasping and pounding the surface of the quilt with her fists.

He stayed with her, continuing his intimate caress, amplifying the pleasure for her... and for him. Her moans of satisfaction eased his mind, if not his cock.

As her muscles relaxed, he slipped his hands free and nuzzled his way back, pausing to lick dewy moisture from her soft skin. "You're delicious."

She dragged in a breath. "And you're relentless."

"Want me to take one of those back?" Balanced on his forearms, he enjoyed his first glimpse of a post-orgasmic Faye. He'd never seen her look this relaxed, not even when she'd been toasted. He took some pride in being a significant part of the experience that had left her so happy she was glowing.

"I'm not sure how that would work."

"It wouldn't. I was just being a smartass. You're stuck with two climaxes in a row. Deal with it."

"I'm pretty sure I did." She smiled. "That's what you get when you make love to a woman who knows how to project."

"Yeah, that was fun." He loved listening to her talk. Naturally she sounded good. She was a singer. But it was more than that. He liked her choice of words, her way of assembling them.

"Now if you'll be so kind as to let me up, I'll return the favor."

He sucked in a breath as his cock responded with enthusiasm to that suggestion.

Her smile widened. "Alrighty, then. Just roll over and—" The theme from *Bonanza* made her blink. "Is that your phone?"

"Yes, ma'am." He winced as he sat back on his heels and reached for the phone lying on the edge of the quilt. "It's my mother."

12

Faye scrambled to grab her clothes, her heart racing as if Gil's mother had suddenly appeared.

Gil took a breath and tapped the phone "Hey, Mom. What's up?"

She turned away and swallowed a giggle as she pulled on her clothes.

"She *is*? Holy shit!"

Faye's attention swung back to him. Awww. Gil looked like the little boy in *A Christmas Story* right after he'd been given a Red Ryder rifle. She made a calculated guess as to the reason. He was talking fast, another clue.

"Yeah, yeah, we're um...finished with lunch." He gave Faye a glance.

She responded with a thumbs-up.

"We can be there in—" He paused. "Oh, okay. You're right. If her contractions are that far apart, it'll be a while. In any case we'll see you soon. Great news." He tapped the phone and tucked it in his pocket.

"Which one is it?"

"Kendall. She and Cheyenne are at the hospital." Excitement vibrated in his voice.

"Woo-hoo! Is your mom there, too?"

"She decided to wait for us so we can all ride in together."

"We?"

"Well, yeah." He peered at her. "Why not?"

She could think of a couple of reasons, but Gil's brother was about to become a dad. A new McLintock would soon enter the world, making Gil an uncle once again. He likely didn't have the bandwidth for anything else. "Let's get going." She pulled her T-shirt over her head. "We'll talk on the way."

"Okay." Shirt hanging open, he started packing up the remnants of their lunch.

She enjoyed the view as she sat down and pulled on her boots. "I don't think I thanked you."

"For the lunch?" He flashed her a grin.

"And the treat afterward. It was a heck of a way to break my celibacy streak."

"Oh, yeah?" He screwed the top on the thermos. "How long?"

"About five months, give or take."

"Anything serious?"

"Might have been. He turned in his resignation so he could leave for New York at the end of the semester. I could either quit and go with him or break it off. I broke it off."

"Good. He wasn't right for you." Putting the satchel and thermos on the grass, he reached for his boots and hat.

"How can you tell? You've never met him."

"I know his kind. Charts a course, plows ahead, doesn't care if he knocks a few things over along the way."

"Singlemindedness helps in that world."

"I'm sure it does. Doesn't leave much room for considering others, though."

"True. Anyway, how long—" She stopped herself, but not in time. "You don't have to answer that."

"But I will. I have you beat. Six months."

"Serious?"

"She was." He stood and buttoned his shirt. "She pushed for a commitment after we'd only dated about three months. I wasn't there yet. She got mad and started dating someone else. Their wedding was the first Saturday in July."

"Good grief. We each dodged a bullet."

"I'm getting good at it."

She laughed. "Me, too. Let's fold up this quilt." She picked up two corners.

"Let's do." Setting the satchel and thermos on the grass, he took the corners on the other side.

She glanced at him across the colorful expanse. "Great quilt."

He smiled. "Better than the scratchy old army blanket from my twin bed at home?"

"I didn't notice it was scratchy." She walked toward him. "I was too busy noticing you, naked."

"Ditto." He met her holding his side of the blanket. "Got a kiss for me?"

"I might be able to find one around here somewhere." Stepping closer, the blanket tucked between them, she stood on tiptoe and leaned in, aiming for his mouth. She missed and got his chin. "This is harder than I thought."

"Hold still. I've got this." Tilting his head, he captured her mouth. "Mmm."

"Mm-hm." He tasted of sex, and wow, did that turn her on... and affect her balance. With a little squeak, she staggered backward but righted herself at the last minute. "Still got the quilt!" She held up both corners in triumph.

He laughed and closed the distance between them. "Nice save. I should have kissed you instead."

"Nah, it was a fun challenge. If I'd kept up my yoga I could have pulled it off." She matched her corners to his and they kept folding the quilt lengthwise until it was narrow enough to roll.

"You stopped doing yoga?" He tucked the rolled quilt under his arm. "I thought you loved that."

"I did. I do." Hoisting the satchel over her shoulder, she picked up the thermos and headed for the grazing horses. "But there are only so many hours in the day."

"You must be putting on a lot of plays."

"We are, and that's the fun part. I also spend a fair amount of time writing grant proposals. Turns out I'm good at it."

"Doesn't sound like your favorite, though."

"Not compared to teaching classes and directing productions, but grants are important. The money allows us to update equipment and stage performances we couldn't afford otherwise."

"They're lucky to have you."

She glanced at him. "Nice of you to say. I feel like the lucky one. I wanted to stay in Montana.

It was one of the reasons I decided to teach. The thought of living anywhere else...."

"I can't imagine it. Just look at our mountains." He swept a hand toward the mountains.

"The Sapphires. I guess that kind of makes them ours."

"I secretly feel that way." His gaze lingered on the blue-green ridges thrusting into a cloudless sky.

Her focus shifted from the mountains to the man. They provided the perfect backdrop for Gil. He'd looked good as Danny, but she preferred this version — his work Stetson pulled low to shade his eyes, his wear-softened shirt tucked into jeans faded by many washings, and his boots scuffed from countless hours on the job shoeing horses.

He turned, catching her in groupie mode. "Do I pass inspection?"

"You'll do."

He laughed. "Let's get a move on." Strapping the quilt behind his saddle, he gathered the reins and mounted up. "Since you're leading, feel free to pick up the pace."

"Roger that." She set off at a trot which became a canter once she reached the path. Anything faster would put her and the horse at risk, but a canter was reasonably safe, especially since Pie and Dollar knew this route well.

If they were in a movie, cantering through the trees with Gil would be a transition scene, one with a rich soundtrack and filters on the lens to create a soft-focus, romantic mood.

But this wasn't a romance and she'd better not pretend that it was. She'd been his first lover, but she wouldn't be his last.

If she let that bother her, then she might as well call off this deal once they'd brushed the horses and turned them loose in the pasture. But what kind of fool would cancel an amazing week of sex, laughter and chocolate chip cookies?

Not her. She'd make the smart move and drop the curtain on Gil's future sex life while she enjoyed the vignette she'd signed up for.

<u>13</u>

Once Gil pointed his horse toward home, he quickly figured out why Faye had been hesitant about riding to the hospital with his mom. "I'll bet when you proposed this new plan you didn't expect to be thrown into a family gathering this afternoon."

"I didn't. But now that I've had time to think about it, I'm glad it's worked out this way."

"Why's that?"

"I want to be part of the excitement. I wish I'd come down for the double-duty baby shower but—"

"Yeah, Ella said the end of the semester was kicking your butt."

"Uh-huh." Which hadn't exactly been true.

"Or was it because you knew I'd be there?"

She sighed. "Yep."

"At least you showed up last August, when Ella almost married that dirtbag."

"You tried to have a conversation with me then. I wasn't very nice to you."

"It's okay."

"Not really. There was no excuse for behaving that way toward you. I'm sorry. I'm glad you stuck with it this time."

"You are, huh?" He couldn't help grinning. "Wonder why?"

"For your information, I'm *not* talking about those two orgasms."

"I know. Just teasing you. But they sure didn't hurt my cause."

"No, they didn't." Laughter rippled in her voice.

"I wish I could see your face. I'll bet you're blushing."

"If I am, I'd better blush and get it over with because I don't want to act the least bit embarrassed when the word gets out about us."

"And it will, eventually. We can't keep it secret."

"That's another reason for me to go to the hospital. It could be the perfect place to subtly handle the reveal."

He gulped. "Today? In the waiting room?"

"Do you think that's a bad idea?"

"Not bad, exactly, but what's the rush?" Maybe he wasn't as cool about this development as he imagined.

"The longer we wait, the more likely someone will notice something's different. I'm tired of keeping this secret."

His stomach hurt. "You want to tell them about Senior Ditch Day, too?"

"Not today, and not ever for some people."

The tightness in his gut eased. "You have the right to, though. I didn't mean to sound so horrified."

"Don't worry. When I tell Ella, and I probably will someday, you'll come out as a hero."

He snorted. "Some hero."

"You brought condoms. You were kind and gentle. That's heroic. But that story can stay in the vault for now. I'd like to make our current situation public, though."

"I don't want to steal Cheyenne and Kendall's thunder. Theirs and baby whozit's."

"I don't, either. I don't think we will, though. I don't think we even could if we wanted to. That baby's birth is so center stage that we should be able to slip in our tiny drama without making much of a splash."

"How?"

"What if I get Ella aside and tell her about us, and you find a moment to talk with Bret? Those two should be the first to know."

"I agree with you there. Bret would be hurt if he heard it from someone other than me."

"Same with Ella."

"Okay, so we split up and start with them. What do we say?"

"Before we spill the beans, we emphasize that although it's not a secret, they're the only ones we're telling for now. But they're free to pass it on or not. Up to them."

"They'll pass it on. Might not take long since everyone will be together. But how do we describe this... whatever we're doing?"

"I'm working on it."

"Let's not call it an affair. Or worse yet, a no-strings affair."

"Yeah, your brother is marrying my sister, so we'll have strings. Loose strings, but they'll exist."

"Or a fling. That one's even more stupid than affair. I picture people tossing each other around like acrobats."

"Yeah, it's dumb."

"*Affair* sounds like you're doing something you should feel guilty about and *fling* sounds like you don't give a damn about the other person. Words matter."

"You don't have to tell me. Words are my stock in trade. Let me think about it."

"Take your time." Being with Faye had been easy ten years ago, at least until that fateful night. Now that they'd sorted through the crap, it was becoming easy again. He liked that. He liked *her*. Under different circumstances, he'd—

"How about we say something simple? Like although we have chemistry, our lives would never mesh. But we happen to be together this week, so we've decided to indulge ourselves."

"Hm." He repeated the two sentences a couple of times. "So this is an indulgence?"

"I guess you could say that."

"Indulgence. Like a piece of the Buffalo's chocolate layer cake. A treat. I like it."

"I do, too, but as for the rest of it, don't feel you have to use those exact words."

"I'm using those words. They're better than anything I'd come up with. No wonder they've saddled you with writing grant proposals. You're good at expressing yourself."

"I'm not saddled. I'm happy that I can help bring in money."

"Sounds nice, but something in your voice tells me it's a burden."

"It's not." Her tone made it clear she was done with that topic. "So why is Kendall at the hospital? Didn't she want a home birth?"

Had he touched on a sore point? Could be, but he'd let it go. "That plan changed about a week ago."

"How come?"

"At her last checkup, Doc Bradley, aka your dad, advised against it. The baby's head isn't facing down so it'll be a little trickier."

"Then I'm glad she's at the hospital, but I'm not worried. My dad's handled quite a few breech births. He's convinced that women usually don't need a caesarian."

"Kendall doesn't want one unless there's no choice. Last I heard she planned to do something called an upright birth."

"Yep, that's my dad's specialty. Kendall's in good hands."

"She knows that." The gate was just ahead. In a few moments they'd be in sight of the ranch. "Hold up. And scoot Pie over. I'm coming alongside."

"Oh?" She pulled back on the reins and turned in the saddle. "What for? As if I didn't know."

"It might be a long time before I can do this again." He guided Dollar forward until the tip of his boot aligned with the tip of hers. His need to savor her mouth one more time warned him that he was in trouble. What else was new?

Grinning, she took off her hat, hooked it on the saddle horn and leaned toward him, her gray eyes alight with anticipation.

So beautiful. *Our lives will never mesh.* His throat ached with longing.

She ran her tongue slowly over her perfect mouth. "Got a kiss for me, cowboy?"

"Yes, ma'am." He sounded like a mating bullfrog. Appropriate. He nudged back his hat, met her halfway and cupped the back of her head, shoving his fingers into the silken luxury of her hair. "I promise not to make it too hot." His galloping heart gave the lie to that promise. "Can't have you blushing as we ride in."

"Aw, give it your best shot. I can recover before your mom sees me."

Heat surged through him. "Alrighty, then." He tightened his fingers, tilted her head a tiny bit and took possession of that glistening mouth.

Ahhh. In the first seconds he was always engulfed in a wave of sensuality, and now the wave had gained power from what had happened in the meadow. Plunging his tongue deep brought a soft moan of need from her throat, a faint echo of the joyous cries of release that still rang in his ears.

She clutched his shoulders, her fingers digging in, her breathing ragged. And he was back in the meadow, caressing, tasting, dazzled by the banquet that was Faye.

He groaned, torn by conflicting desires. He wanted to be in that waiting room when Cheyenne's firstborn arrived. He did. But he also yearned to lie in a king-sized bed with this incredible woman and make love until they were exhausted.

She pulled back, gasping. "We have to stop or—"

"I know." He swallowed. "Thank you. I'm not sure I would have—"

"It's okay." She patted his heaving chest and breathed deep. "We just… it'll be good when we can finally—"

"Wear each other out?"

"Tell me about it. I had the appetizer. Now I want—"

"We'll get there."

"I have no room to complain. You're the one who must be suffering something fierce."

He shifted in the saddle. "It's my own fault. I'm the one who had to have a kiss to tide me over."

"Are you tided?"

"No, I'm worse off." He glanced at her. "You?"

"Same."

"Sorry. Bad idea."

"Good idea. Bad timing." Straightening, she plucked her hat from the saddle horn and settled it on her head. "How long before you'll be ready to ride?"

"Sixty seconds." He gazed at the mountains instead of focusing on her sexy self. "Works like a charm." A minute later he took a deep breath and let it out. "Let me text Mom and tell her we're almost at the gate." He tapped on his phone and tucked it back in his pocket. "Let's ride."

"Alrighty." She urged Pie forward with a soft click of her tongue. "So looking at the mountains is your trick?"

"Actually, it's been years since I've had this problem."

"How many years?"

"Oh, about ten."

"Don't tell me I'm the only one who's ever gotten a rise out of you. I'll know you're lying."

"Of course you're not the only one. From puberty through eleventh grade sex was all I could think about. Didn't take much to get me excited back then. I perfected the art of boner control the summer between my junior and senior year. I was golden. And then… then you came along."

14

Faye didn't know how to process Gil's confession. He could control his sexual reaction to other women but not to her? What did that mean? And did she even want to know? His reaction to her was unusual but it didn't mean she was his soul mate. Right?

"You don't believe me."

"That's just it. I do believe you. You have no reason to lie about something so personal. But won't that create a problem this week?"

"No, because the mountains are visible from just about everywhere. It's why it was my go-to in high school."

"Huh. Smart." She rode up to the gate, and Pie stood quietly while she leaned down, lifted the latch and swung the gate wide. If she were Desiree, she'd be at the barn to greet them and help with the horses. Sure enough, as they approached, she came out of the barn carrying a grooming tote.

And Faye was suddenly eighteen again. Although it was broad daylight, the presence of Gil's mother felt eerily like when she'd come home in the wee hours from Senior Ditch Day and her mother had met her at the door.

"Hi, Ms. McLintock!" She leaned hard on her acting skills and hoped to hell she sounded more relaxed than she felt. "Great news, huh?" She dismounted quickly.

"Fabulous news. And you can call me Desiree, now, remember?"

"Right, right. Sorry. Thanks for waiting for us."

"Seemed logical since you were on your way back."

"Are Buck and Marybeth going in with us, too?" Bonus, a ride with three parental figures.

"They decided to have lunch at the Buffalo today so they're already there. It's only me."

"Well, I'm sure you're eager to get going." She looped the reins around the hitching post to the right of the barn door as Gil guided Dollar in next to Pie. "Thanks for bringing out the tote. We'll—"

"Might go faster if I groom Pie. I'll bet you could use a restroom before we make the drive in. I'll take care of Pie."

"Um, okay, thanks. I accept that offer." Did she look like she'd been rolling around on a quilt with Gil? Was that why Desiree had suggested a trip to the house? No. She was being paranoid.

Except Desiree's glance of motherly concern was doggone familiar, a lot like the one Faye's mom had given her all those years ago. She'd said *glad you're home safe*, kissed her on the cheek and hustled her off to bed.

Faye exchanged a quick glance with Gil and made tracks for the house, her face warm, her thoughts jumbled. Nothing in Desiree's manner indicated disapproval. She liked Faye and her son was a grown man.

But how would she react when she learned the relationship would be short and sweet? Logically she'd be fine with it. Her lifestyle had been all about temporary liaisons.

Hurrying up the porch steps, she crossed the porch, opened the large wooden door and stepped inside. Sam ran to greet her, feathery tail wagging.

"Hey, Sam." Crouching down, she gave him a good scratch. Then she wrapped both arms around him and buried her face in his ruff. "You're lucky you're a dog. Human lives are so complicated."

"Second thoughts?"

Lifting her head, she glanced behind her. She'd left the door open when she'd crouched down to pet Sam. Gil stood just inside, his broad shoulders blocking the light, the satchel over his shoulder.

He thumbed back his hat. "You can still back out. Nobody has to know what happened in the meadow."

"Did your mom ask you about it?"

"No. She just wondered if we had anything that should go in the fridge."

"I think she has a pretty good idea we're involved."

"Yeah, but she doesn't know for sure. We can scrap the plan. As long as we keep our cool, she won't poke into it."

His words gave her a way out, but she didn't want out. The kindness in his gentle voice rekindled the longing she hadn't begun to satisfy. Giving Sam a final scratch, she stood and faced him. "I don't want to scrap the plan. We have unfinished business."

The corners of his mouth tipped up. "Interesting turn of phrase."

"Well, don't we?"

"Yes, ma'am. But we could postpone talking to Ella and Bret."

"If we don't get the word out today, I'll feel like we're sneaking around. I'd rather be open with both our families. After this baby is born, whenever that turns out to be, I assume we'll go back to your cabin."

"We'd have to. Your car's there."

"And if I have anything to say about it, my car will stay there until you kick me out. I'd rather have your family know in advance why it's there."

Heat flickered in his blue eyes. "Alrighty, then."

"Now if you'll excuse me, I'll go avail myself of the facilities and find out if I have leaves in my hair."

"You don't. I would have said something. You look fine." His gaze softened. "More than fine. You look beautiful."

Her breath caught.

"But then, you always do."

"Thank you." She swallowed. "That's… nice to hear."

"I've never told you before?"

"No." She would have remembered.

"I should have. I've thought it enough times." He swallowed. "You'd better skedaddle before I kiss you."

"Yeah, okay." She hurried away, smiling. Although she didn't define herself by her looks, being told she was beautiful by a man she craved was heady stuff. The glow from this short conversation should carry her through whatever happened in the hospital waiting room.

Ten minutes later she was riding shotgun in Desiree's big purple truck as they pulled away from the ranch house. Gil had taken the spot in the back behind the driver's seat. If Faye turned her head slightly to the left, he appeared in her peripheral vision.

Whenever she looked, he was looking back. *Because he thinks I'm beautiful.* What a concept.

Now that they were on their way, Desiree's calm patience had clearly gone bye-bye. She gunned the engine and left a rooster tail of dust on the dirt roads she owned.

Faye glanced back at Gil, who merely shrugged and smiled. If he wasn't going to comment on his mother's driving, Faye wasn't about to.

"Okay." Desiree braked as they reached the turn onto the paved road leading into town. "That felt great." She took a deep breath. "But I can't drive like that the rest of the way or I'm liable to attract a smoky."

Faye was enjoying this glimpse into a side of Desiree she hadn't been privy to. "Maybe not. It's Sunday. The road's deserted."

"I see that." She threw both hands in the air. "I'm getting another grandbaby!"

"I forgot to ask," Gil said. "Do you get to be in the room? I know Angie will be."

"Kendall asked me to, and I'm so honored. Shouldn't be as scary as Jess having Maverick, but just as exciting. I feel like I'm strapped into a roller coaster, itching to start the ride."

"Then go for it, Mom. Faye and I will keep an eye out."

"Yeah, Wayne's good at hiding in the bushes. Just my luck he'll be tucked in somewhere along this stretch and I'll have to waste time talking myself out of a ticket. We need us a discussion. That'll slow me down. Whatcha got, guys?"

Faye laughed. "Improv time?"

"Exactly. Name a topic."

"The fire department's bachelor auction."

"Good one." Desiree gave her an approving glance. "Son, you start. I'll jump in whenever you leave something out."

"Guaranteed I will." Gil launched into an account of Clint taking Cheyenne's place on stage.

"Did he fool Kendall?"

"Not for a second." Desiree kept the truck moving at the posted speed limit. "She out-bid everyone, took Cheyenne home with her and fed him sugar cookies. She's been crazy about him since she was three, but he wouldn't give her the time of day."

"Why? She's amazing."

"He realizes that now," Desiree said. "But he shied away because she was too young, at least in his mind, and he figured she had zero experience. Which turned out to be true. He was her first."

"Oh. Wow." Faye didn't look at Gil. "That first time can be awkward."

"Turns out it wasn't in that case." Desiree continued her steady pace. "It was great."

"Oh. Well, good, then."

"But Cheyenne thought she deserved a chance to play the field." Gil said. "They wrangled with that, but as you can see, they came to an understanding."

"And now they're having my grandbaby!" Desiree stomped on the gas again, throwing Faye back against the seat. "Whoops. Sorry. More talk, more talk. Gil, tell her about Angie and Dallas. You were sort of involved with that."

"Um, I was. In a way." He sounded reluctant.

A quick glance confirmed it. A flush stained his tanned neck and face. Was he still feeling guilty about telling Dallas their Senior Ditch Day secret?

Maybe. He didn't look at her as he described Angie's reaction to Dallas at the auction, which jump-started her long-range plan to rope in that firefighter.

"The point is, we didn't know she was serious about him and had thought it through." Gil's voice took on a defensive tone. "And he's six years older and he was planning to buy Cheyenne's cabin, so some of us were... concerned that the relationship wasn't a good idea."

Desiree gave a snort.

Faye glanced at her in surprise. "You weren't concerned?"

"Not about Angie and Dallas."

Ah. Maybe Gil's guilt went a little deeper. Clearly there was more to the story, actions taken that had displeased his mother. Faye chose to steer the conversation in a different direction. "Did Dallas buy Cheyenne's place?"

Desiree shook her head. "He gave up on that when he realized how much he loves Angie's cabin. And now that his brother's coming to Montana, he's going to rent it from Cheyenne."

"Seems like a lot of things are bubbling under the surface at Rowdy Ranch."

Desiree laughed. "Sweetie, you have no idea."

"There's more?"

"Oh, yeah. But we're out of time." She swung into the parking lot of Wagon Train's hospital.

The one-story structure was modest by city standards, but Faye viewed it with affection, probably because her dad praised it as *the best little hospital in Montana.*

"Oh, good," Desiree switched off the engine and opened her door. "Andy just pulled in. You guys go ahead." She hopped down and hurried over to a gray pickup several spots away. *The Wagon Train Sentinel* was lettered on the doors.

Gil came around the back of Desiree's truck just as Faye was climbing out. She waited so he could help her. "You don't need to do this, you know."

"But I like doing this. Thanks for humoring me." He gave her hand a squeeze.

She glanced into those mesmerizing blue eyes and gulped. Yeah, she'd grab any chance to touch this man. But now wasn't the time to dwell on his attributes. "Hey, why is your mom so stoked that Andy's here? Is she angling for a big feature story on her grandbaby?"

Gil chuckled. "You really are out of the loop." He let go of her hand and gestured toward the hospital entrance.

She matched his stride as they walked toward the glass double doors. "So fill me in."

"Well, since Kendall's lost both parents, Mom's doing double duty in the grandmother role and Andy's offered to take on grandfather duties."

"That's sweet. I mean, he's Maverick's actual grandfather, so he might as well step in as the honorary grandpa for this little one, too."

"Yep. That's what he said."

"Why are you smiling?"

"Because you still don't get it."

"Get what?"

"Andy's got a crush on Mom."

"Oooohhhh." She glanced over her shoulder toward the gray truck where Desiree and Andy were laughing about something. "That's adorable."

"What's even more adorable is that she's got a crush on him, too, but she won't admit it. According to her, they're just *good friends*." He wiggled his fingers to make air quotes.

"Now I'm sad that I'm not around more. That would be fun to watch."

"So come around more."

She paused and looked at him, at a loss for how to respond.

"Never mind. Let's go in."

15

Gil was irritated with himself. Hours into this arrangement and he'd already mucked it up by suggesting Faye spend more time in Wagon Train. She'd been clear about what she wanted — a week of fun and games with a rock-solid end point.

He kept quiet as they walked into the hospital. She didn't say anything either. Odds were she was mulling over his stupid-ass remark and reconsidering her decision.

Right before they reached the reception desk, he muttered a quick *I'm sorry.*

"Don't worry about it," she said under her breath.

The reception area was small, but light and airy all the same. Background country music blended with the buzz of conversation and the sparkle of laughter drifting down the hall from the waiting room.

The builders had recognized that a small hospital in a small town still required a large waiting room. Whether for a happy event like this one or a crisis when a life hung in the balance, a truckload of friends and family would gather.

Sherry, the sixty-something woman who worked the reception desk on weekends, got up and came around to give Faye a big hug. She beamed at Gil and hugged him, too.

That startled him a bit since he didn't know her very well, or the weekday receptionist, either, since he hardly ever had a reason to come in here. But naturally Doc Bradley's daughter would know the staff, some of them probably for years.

Sherry was clearly overjoyed to see her. "I was hoping to run into you before Saturday and look, here you are with your Danny! How cute is that?"

Gil blinked. "You remember the show?"

"Honey, I went to all three performances. Leslie was in it."

"Oh, right." Leslie's mom. He hadn't made the connection. "How's she doing? I haven't seen her since the five-year reunion." When he'd prayed she wouldn't agree to sing with him.

"Great, great. She and Jerry have a carpet and tile store in Billings that's going gangbusters. They'll be coming to the ten-year reunion in October. Faye, are you going to make it? Leslie told me you didn't come to the five-year."

"I missed it, but I've promised Gil I'll be at this one."

"Wonderful! I'll tell Leslie. She'll be tickled. But I'd better warn you, they'll want you to sing."

"That's okay. I think I can talk Gil into doing *Summer Nights*."

"At the wedding?" His mom approached, Andy right behind her. She frowned in confusion. "I thought you were singing *When You Say Nothing at All*?"

"I am," Faye said. "We're talking about the ten-year reunion."

"Oh! Sorry. That's what I get for coming in at the tail end of the discussion." She grinned. "Adding a rendition of *Summer Nights* would be kinda fun, though." Her eyes took on a familiar gleam. "But I doubt Ella wants to mess with the wedding program at this late date. On the other hand, since I'm in charge of the rehearsal dinner at the Buffalo...Faye, what do you think?"

Her eyes held the exact same gleam as his mother's. "I've never performed at the Buffalo. I've always kind of wanted to."

"Great! Gil, you'll sing it with her, won't you?"

He hesitated.

"It'll come back to you. I'll bet you'd only need a couple of run-throughs."

That wasn't the problem. He'd do just fine. Was he as good as he used to be? He couldn't tell since he practiced alone. He'd kept it to himself just in case Bret might view those sessions as evidence that he'd sacrificed a theater career to honor his promise.

"We need more than Gil," Faye said. "*Summer Nights* requires backup singers."

His mom gestured toward the waiting room. "You have a pool of talent right down that hall. Rance and Clint would do it in a heartbeat. Angie, too. I'll bet Tyra would, and that's just for starters. It's a great idea. C'mon. Time to check on that baby." She led the way.

He and Faye followed.

"Don't worry." She kept her voice down. "We'll run through it a couple of times this week."

"It's not that. I'll do okay. It's just...never mind. I'll work it out."

"Trust me, we'll have fun." She gave him a smile as they approached the waiting room door. "Ready to work our plan?"

He paused. "Shoot, I almost forgot about that." He sucked in a breath. "Yeah, I'm ready."

"We'll have to split up once we get in there. But come find me after you've talked to Bret."

"I will."

His mom and Andy walked in ahead of them to cries of *Grandma and Grandpa are here!*

When he and Faye stepped in, she started giggling. "I'm so glad at least one of the babies decided to be born while I was here. This is nuts."

"When you're right, you're right." He took in the balloons and crepe paper streamers, enough of both to decorate a carnival midway.

"I see they decided against going all pink."

"Kendall and Cheyenne want their baby to be surrounded by a bunch of different colors. If she ends up liking pink, fine, but she gets a choice. Anyway, I hope somebody's taking pictures of this. It's a whole different vibe from Maverick's coming out party."

"I doubt hanging around in the front yard of Beau's place lends itself to balloons and streamers."

"Clearly this setting does." He took another breath and scanned the room. His mom had gone back to check on Kendall. Angie was nowhere in sight, so she must be back there, too.

Although chairs and couches were available, everyone had chosen to stand. Clint and Tyra had plenty of helpers as they set up self-serve jugs of iced tea, lemonade and apple cider. Rance supervised the unloading of sandwiches and desserts from the Buffalo onto another table.

Bret and a noticeably pregnant Molly stood talking with Beau and Jess on the opposite side of the room. They were probably keeping their kids away from the food prep, since Zach and Maverick played on the floor at their feet, building and knocking down towers of blocks.

Faye glanced around. "At least Ella's on one side of the room and Bret's on the other. It would have been awkward if they'd been hanging out together."

"Correction. *More* awkward. This is way out of my comfort zone."

"You can still—"

"No, ma'am. We're doing this." He held her gaze for another second. "See you soon."

"Same here. Good luck." She brushed his hand and walked away.

Heart racing, he started toward Bret, moving fast, concentrating on his reasons for doing this crazy thing.

Bret would have to be in a group that included Beau, the guy who could give him a hard time about asking for a private conversation. Nobody hated being out of the loop more than Beau.

Sure enough, he called out to him as he approached. "There he is. How was your picnic?"

So Beau had dug out that intel. "Fun." Understatement of the century.

Jess gave him a smile. "I was surprised when Beau told me you went riding with Faye this afternoon. I didn't know you were close. But then he reminded me about *Grease*. I'm sorry I missed it."

"Excellent show." Beau's gaze moved over Gil, assessing. "Didn't know my little brother had it in him."

"I read my dad's review since he sent me every issue while I was in Pennsylvania," Jess said. "He raved."

"It was a nice writeup." He shifted his weight and wrestled with how to play this. He was a silver-tongued devil when schmoozing customers for McLintock Metalworks. But that skill had deserted him in this situation.

Then Jess fed him the perfect line. "You two probably have a lot of memories to share, huh?"

"We do. We have. Great memories." He looked over at Bret, who was eyeing him, his expression a perfect match for Beau's. "In fact, while we were reminiscing, something came up. I'd like to discuss it with Bret, if you'll excuse us for a minute." *Something came up*? Sheesh. Hilarious, except he was too nervous to laugh at himself.

Bret nodded and stepped away from the group. "We'll be out on the patio. Come get us if you hear anything."

"Will do. Let me know if you need another view on the matter." Beau's curiosity had to be killing him. He looked ready to explode.

Bret led the way to a walled patio shaded in the late afternoon by an oak on the far side of the wall. He pushed open the glass door and paused to look back at Gil. "Faye and Ella are out here."

"Oh. Then maybe—"

"Hey, guys," Ella called. "Come join us. Something tells me we're all here for the same reason, so we might as well talk about it together."

Bret glanced at Gil.

"Sure. Why not?" If Ella was suggesting it, then who was he to disagree with his future sister-in-law?

Faye and Ella sat across from each other at one of two wooden picnic tables with attached benches. They scooted over to make room. Gil took the spot next to Faye and Bret climbed in next to Ella.

Ella turned to Bret. "We just got started, so to catch you up I've learned that my sister is attracted to your brother and vice-versa."

Bret smiled. "Still? Did I just step into a time warp?"

"I know, right? Ten years ago my folks were terrified they'd run off and get married."

"So was Mom. But instead..." He fixed Gil with a steady gaze. "Something must have happened."

"Clearly." Ella looked hard at Faye.

How much did these two suspect? Gil nudged Faye's knee under the table. "It was my fault. I loused things up between us."

Faye nudged back. "We were very young. And headed in different directions, which we still are. Not young, but the different directions thing is the same. That said, there's this pesky chemistry between us."

"I had a feeling that was the issue," Ella said. "You've been so manic about avoiding him. I wondered what you'd do about the wedding. Marsh and I talked about it."

Gil looked across the table at his brother. "How about you? Did you wonder what was going on with me and Faye?"

"I noticed she's been conspicuously absent from any gathering that includes you, but I don't know her as well as Marsh does. And since you never mention her, I figured you'd done something unforgivable, something so bad you were ashamed to tell me."

Heat rose to his cheeks. "You're not far off."

"Yes, he is!" Faye bumped his shoulder and scowled at him. "Nothing you did was unforgivable. I won't have them thinking that. We wouldn't be sitting here if you hadn't been determined to make things right between us."

"I take it he succeeded." Ella focused on her sister.

Faye's cheeks turned pink. "Yes. Which brings us to why we wanted to talk with you and Bret. We want you to be the first to hear—"

"You're getting *married*?" Ella jerked back as if she'd been hit in the face with a cream pie.

"No! The exact opposite!"

Bret frowned. "You can't get divorced if you're not—"

"You've been *secretly* married?" Ella's voice rose another notch. "All this time?"

"We're not married," Gil said. "That's the point. We'll never be married." Depressing concept, but he soldiered on, reaching for the words Faye had come up with. "Between her work at UM and mine down here, our lives will never mesh. They're... well... unmeshable."

Bret stared at him. "Is that even a word?"

"If it's not, it should be."

"But the wedding brought us together for this one week," Faye said. "And we'll be around each other a lot, even more than we thought because Desiree wants us to perform *Summer Nights* at the rehearsal."

"Sounds like fun," Ella said. "Is the performance a secret? Although that doesn't seem like something Bret and I specifically have to—"

"It's not about the performance, it's about us, and that's not a secret, either." Gil remembered that part was supposed to come before anything else. Blew that call. "We don't care who knows, but we want you guys to be the first to hear it."

Ella's eyes snapped with impatience. "The first to hear *what*?"

Bret put a hand on her arm. "I think maybe they're trying to tell us they're having an affair."

"Oh!" Ella's eyes widened. "Why didn't you just say so?"

"Not an affair," Gil said. "It's—"

"A fling, then?" She still looked disoriented.

He shook his head. "Not that, either." But what had they decided to call it? He turned to Faye, his mind a blank.

By now her cheeks were very pink. "We're going to indulge ourselves."

"That's it." Gil turned back to Ella and Bret. "We're going to have an indulgence."

16

"I thought that went well." Gil handed Faye a glass of iced tea from one of the jugs Clint and Tyra had hauled in from the Buffalo.

"You did?" She managed not to laugh because he looked endearingly sincere.

"You didn't?"

"I thought it was a fustercluck. But maybe that was better than if we'd made a polished presentation. It's an emotional topic. We should be a little rattled when we talk about it."

"Yeah, okay, I was rattled."

"Me, too, and I was so sure my training would kick in."

"You did great. You remembered *indulge*. I couldn't think of it to save my soul." He glanced around the room. "Do you think the word's getting out?"

"I'm sure our *indulgence* has torn through this crowd like wildfire. Haven't you noticed the furtive glances our way? And the fact that no one's come to get snacks and drinks ever since we moved to this part of the room?"

"So everyone's going to ignore us?"

"Of course not, but for now they need to talk among themselves. I'm glad your mom popped back in to grab something to drink. I didn't want her to be the first to know, but I sure wouldn't want her to be the last, either."

"Seems like Kendall, Cheyenne, Angie and your dad will be the last."

"Could be. But that's okay. Mom's the right person to break the news to Dad later, when he's not shepherding this baby into the world."

"Kendall and Cheyenne will be oblivious for days. I remember how Beau and Jess were after Mav was born. A giant asteroid could have been heading for Earth and they wouldn't have cared."

"Angie won't care if she doesn't hear about us until later. She's right where she wants to be."

"That's for sure. I'm glad it's going well in there."

"I knew it would, since Dad's a big fan of the upright birth method."

"Yeah. And I just realized I never questioned that term. I can't imagine she just stands there and lets the baby drop out."

"No, but she's not in a bed, either. She's either squalling or sitting. It's far more natural than the standard way we do it in our culture. If I have kids, I'm doing it like that, even if they're not breach."

"I'd never heard of it until this time with Kendall. You'd think with Mom having nine, I would have."

"You know, I think my dad delivered some of..." She stared at him. "He said he delivered her last three, which means—"

"He delivered me. I knew that. Mom told us that he took over for a doctor who retired, and I was the first one of us he delivered."

"Right. It's coming back to me. He said she had the easiest delivery of any woman he'd had as a patient. She might not have been looking around for a better way since she had no issues."

"Maybe. And maybe she's learning something today, too. When did you hear about this?"

"Years ago. I keep forgetting that most kids don't grow up discussing birthing methods at the dinner table."

"See, that's why I was convinced you weren't..." He paused and glanced around.

"A virgin like you?" She couldn't resist.

He sighed. "Yeah."

"I so wish I'd known it at the time."

"And I so wouldn't have told you. It's tough enough to admit it now. Anyway, you always acted so knowledgeable about... human biology... and stuff."

"I'm a doctor's daughter. Goes with the territory. And by the way, you acted knowledgeable, too."

"Most of that was bravado. I might have known more than some guys because Mom gave it to us straight, but she wasn't big on the technical terms. I overheard you and Tony one time. You were describing the value of a foreskin in sexual pleasure. I had to look it up."

"Do you have one?"

He gave her a wickedly sexy grin. "You don't remember?"

"It was dark. You snapped on the condom before I got a good look."

His grin widened. "I'll be happy to give you a second chance to check that out."

Deep in her core, anticipation uncurled and stretched. "Looking forward to it."

"Me, too. I'm excited about this baby, but..."

"I know."

"I sound like I'm complaining and I'm not. I'll just be glad when she's born and we can head back to—"

"Depending on when it is, I can see your mom throwing an impromptu party at Rowdy Roost."

"Hadn't thought of that. She sure could. Or rather, the Wenches could. They put something together the night Mav was born." He rubbed the back of his neck. "If that happens, we should put in an appearance."

"Of course we should. And we will. Speaking of your mom, she and my mom are headed this way."

"Probably to get a snack."

"I don't think they have snacks in mind."

"Why would they come over together?"

"They each have skin in the game, for one thing, and they may want to present a united front. Sets a precedent for the future."

"But we don't have a future."

An unpleasant fact she'd rather ignore. "They do, though, now that Marsh and Ella are getting married. It's logical they'd form a team." She turned toward the approaching duo. "Hey, Mom! Hey, Desiree! What's up?"

"We've been appointed to come over and reassure you guys that we're all cool with your plan," her mother said as they approached. "Everyone pretty much agrees that it won't work out the way you expect, but—"

"Hey." Faye looked her mother in the eye. "It could."

"It could. I hope it does." She put her hands on Faye's shoulders, gave her a squeeze and let go. "In any case, you get points for your optimistic belief that it will."

"And extra points for labeling it an indulgence." Desiree's gaze moved from him to Faye. "I really like that description. Which one of you thought of it?"

"We came up with it together," Faye said. "But only after Gil rejected the usual words that describe a... short-term relationship."

"Because they're tacky," Gil said.

"You're right, son. And words matter."

Faye smiled. Gil had said the same thing. "I'll bet he learned that from you."

"Hope so. I've said it enough times. Anyway, excellent wordsmithing. You've framed this experiment as a net positive."

Faye blinked. Clearly she hadn't been paying attention all these years. Desiree also had language skills. "That was the idea."

"But what happens when the party's over?"

"That's my question," Liz said. "We all remember how intense you two were on stage ten years ago. Can you just shut that down after seven days? I have my doubts."

Gil squared his shoulders. "With all due respect, we can because we're not eighteen anymore. I know what Faye needs in a partner. I don't fill the bill. I'll back away so she can find that guy."

Faye's chest tightened. "I feel the same way about Gil. He needs a woman who has a job in Wagon Train, who will live in his beautiful cabin, cook with him in that gorgeous kitchen and go riding with him when they have time off." And now she envied that mythical woman so much it made her stomach hurt.

Liz exchanged a look with Desiree. "That sounds very mature."

"Indeed it does." Desiree stepped forward and hugged Gil. "I'm here if you need me."

"Thanks, Mom."

Then she hugged Faye. "I appreciate your openness about this."

"Thanks, Desiree." A weight lifted off her shoulders. She'd made the right call.

Her mom's hug was tighter than Desiree's. "I love you," she murmured.

"Love you, too, Mom." She gulped. She'd received a hug just like this ten years ago.

Letting her go, her mother gave Gil a hug and backed away. "Believe I'll get something to drink."

Gil smiled. "I wish we had something stronger."

Her mom laughed. "You and me both."

As her mom walked away, Faye met Gil's gaze. "You okay?"

"I think so. You?"

"Everyone thinks we'll crash and burn."

"Then we'll just have to prove them wrong, won't we?"

"Perfect response." Her body warmed. "I admire a guy who knows his lines."

"Sometimes. Other times I totally miss my cue."

"Is this the part where I get to kiss you? 'Cause I'd really like to right now."

"Go ahead. It's not like anybody will be shocked."

"No, but a public demonstration might be pushing it. I can wait until—" She paused as Gil's attention shifted. "What now?"

His chest heaved. "Dallas. He's coming over."

"Oh." The only other person in the room who knew the whole story. She'd spotted him early on, but in the flurry of activity she'd lost track of him. "Maybe it's just as well."

Gil lowered his voice. "Faye, I'm sorry. I shouldn't have told him."

"You had your reasons."

"As it turned out they weren't very good reasons."

"You'll have to tell me about it sometime."

"I will." He broke eye contact. "Hey, Dallas. How's it going?"

"Good." He turned toward Faye. "Can I steal this guy for a second? I have something I want—"

"It's okay, dude," Gil said. "She knows I told you. Evidently she's forgiven me."

Dallas let out a breath. "I'm glad. And I want both of you to know that I've said nothing." He zeroed in on Faye. "You can trust me with this."

"I was a little worried you'd let something slip to Angie."

"No, ma'am. I've been very careful about that. I'll carry your secret to the grave."

That made her smile. "I appreciate that, but it won't be necessary. If Gil's okay with it, I'll probably tell Angie myself before too much longer. And my sister, my mom and a few others."

Gil shrugged. "It's time. Not that we'll take out a full-page ad in the *Sentinel*, but now that Faye and I have mended fences…" He looked over at her.

"Yep. We can let it go. Laugh about it, even."

"Well, that's good news," Dallas said. "But until you give me the word, I'll keep quiet. It's your—"

The swinging door to the maternity ward opened with a loud *thwack* and Angie charged through wearing scrubs and looking wild-eyed.

"Mom! Get in here! It's happening!"

Desiree almost knocked her down as she barreled through the opening. "Hang on, baby girl! Grandma's on her way!"

17

Galvanized by Angie's dramatic announcement and his mother's enthusiastic response, Gil scooped Faye into his arms and twirled her around like one of their dance moves from *Grease*. Then he set her down and kissed her, not caring if that was *pushing it*. With all the giddy laughter and cheering going on, who would notice?

The yielding softness of her lips tempted him the way it always did. He wanted more. And when she kissed him back, he took more, burying his fingers in her hair, tilting her head, claiming her mouth with a thrust of his tongue.

She melted into him, her body a perfect fit, her heat setting him on fire. Sliding his hand down to cup her tush, he brought her in tight. Ahh. Sweet torture. The noise of the room faded, drowned out by the thud of his heart vibrating through his head, his chest, his aching groin.

When lack of air made him dizzy, he reluctantly lifted his head and dragged in a breath. So did Faye.

The silence surrounding them registered a second later. Had everybody left? He turned his head to check.

No one had left. They were all very much here, grinning and exchanging glances. Enjoying the show. He looked back at Faye.

Her gaze collided with his and she gasped.

"Easy," he murmured. "We're gonna gracefully separate, hold hands, smile and take a bow."

She pulled in more air. "'kay."

Peeling himself away from her, he blessed the shock of the moment for reducing the evidence. He could turn and face the audience without sporting a ginormous woody. He threaded his fingers through hers and squeezed her hand. She squeezed back.

They executed a classic curtain-call as if they'd done it yesterday — smile, glance at each other, face the audience again, and bow.

Beau whistled through his teeth and began clapping, which set off a wave of applause that didn't show any sign of stopping.

"They love us," he murmured. "They really, really love us."

Faye snorted. "Think we should take another bow?"

"Can't hurt. Ham it up. You curtsy and I'll do the sweeping hand thing."

The second bow brought more whistles, especially when Faye started blowing kisses. Beau took a flower from a nearby vase and tossed it at her feet. Then Rance picked up the entire vase and brought it to her, presenting it on bended knee.

No telling how long the nonsense would have continued if Doc Bradley hadn't pushed through the swinging doors and called out *hey!*

As if a director had yelled *cut*, everyone stopped what they were doing and faced him.

"She's here." His smile took over his entire face. "Josephine Desiree McLintock has arrived. Mother and baby are doing great."

As cheers erupted, Gil gave Faye a sheepish grin. "Not gonna kiss you this time."

"Not gonna let you. Nice save, though."

The doors blasted open again as Angie tore out, her mask under her chin as tears of happiness streamed down her cheeks. "Ohmigod, you guys, she's *gorgeousl.* Looks *exactly* like Kendall. " She swiped at her face. "I'm so h-h-happy!"

Angie hadn't cried in a long time, at least not in Gil's presence. Crying for joy got to him quicker than anything, especially seeing tears on the cheeks of his tough little sis.

His swallow must have been loud enough for Faye to hear. She moved closer and tightened her grip on his hand. "This is beautiful."

"Mm-hm." He didn't trust himself to speak. As everyone rushed forward to pelt Angie with questions, he turned loose of Faye's hand and wrapped his arm around her shoulders, pulling her close. He needed a moment.

His worldview had just shifted. Maverick's birth had been dramatic and moving, but it hadn't punched him in the gut. It hadn't dredged up a yearning he'd refused to acknowledge and poured it over him, drenching him in need.

When Bret had adopted Zach, he'd felt a twinge of envy. Molly's pregnancy had brought another twinge. But nothing like this. He ached all over.

And he wanted. God, how he wanted. Was it a coincidence this fierce longing had taken hold when Faye Bradley was nestled in the curve of his arm? No. A howl of frustration welled in his chest.

She was the one. She'd always been the one. And he'd just promised her mother that in seven days, he would back off so she could find the man of her dreams.

* * *

Sometime later, Cheyenne brought Josephine Desiree to the doorway, holding the swinging doors open with his shoulders so everyone could get a glimpse. They all stayed well back, kept their voices low and used their phones to zoom in on the tiny bundle swaddled so tightly that only her pink face and some wispy brown hair showed.

By then Gil had marshalled his forces and he took a bunch of pictures, too. He'd want them later when he had his act together.

With the main event concluded and a party in the making at Rowdy Roost, the gang dispersed, taking the food and decorations with them. Eventually Gil and Faye were the only ones left in the waiting room.

He glanced at her. "We might as well sit." He gestured toward the nearest couch. "No telling when Mom will be ready to leave."

"Not quite yet, son." She came through the swinging doors, looking mussed and tired, but her eyes shone with happiness. "How about taking the BPT home for me?" She held out the keys.

"Sure, but how will you—"

"Andy. He'll bring me and Angie back when we're able to tear ourselves away. It'll be soon, but I don't want to leave you guys sitting out here when I'm sure you have better things to do." She winked at him.

And he blushed, dammit. "Dallas left? I didn't notice that."

"Angie asked him to go over and take care of the horses and chickens at Cheyenne and Kendall's place."

"Oh. Good call. I totally forgot."

"I think we all did. Cheyenne was prepared to do it, but this is better. It would kill him to have to leave, even for a couple of hours. Anyway, we'll be home soon, I'm sure."

He smiled. "Probably kills you to think of leaving, too."

"Yeah, but I will. They don't really need me. See you later." She gave him a quick hug and looked over at Faye. "See you soon, sweetheart."

"Thank you, Ms.— Desiree."

She laughed, gave them a wave, and went back down the hall.

Returning to Faye with a sense of relief, Gil tossed the keys up and swiped them out of the air. "We're outta here."

"You don't have to say that twice." She kept up with him as they hurried out of the room. "What's a BPT?"

"Big Purple Truck."

"Ha. I should've guessed that. I came up with Brown Paper Towels, which made no sense unless they needed them for the party. Who started calling it the BPT?"

"She did."

"Why?"

"Because it sounds cool."

"Your mom fascinates me."

"She fascinates everyone, including her kids." /

"And Andy."

"Him, too." He shoved open the glass front door and they stepped out into a nearly empty parking lot. Dusk-to-dawn lights flickered as the sky grew pale.

He helped Faye in and closed the door. How many times would he get to do that this week? A paltry dozen, maybe?

He climbed behind the wheel and settled into the luxurious driver's seat. "This thing rides like a limo."

"Do you drive it much?"

"Hardly ever for a distance. Taking it over to the wash pad doesn't count." Turning the key, he brought the powerful engine to life and backed out.

"What an exciting time for your family. A baby today and a wedding next Saturday."

Gil didn't want to think beyond that. Barring a gold-plated miracle, he'd be staring at a lot of nothing. "Stuff's always happening when you choose to have this many kids." And that would likely be his salvation in the coming weeks.

"She told me she absolutely chose to. I remember her saying that she wanted to have all of you. She just never found a man she was willing to marry."

"Except for Sky's dad."

"Oh?"

"She doesn't talk about it much, but she'd be fine with you knowing. Sky's the only one who wasn't planned. She was about to tell the father about the baby when he announced he was in love with someone else."

"I hope she told him anyway."

"She didn't."

"Boy, I would have."

"I think most women would these days. But he was an old-fashioned cowboy and she knew he'd insist on marrying her even though he loved someone else. They'd both be miserable. She kept quiet and moved here."

"Aww. He was the love of her life. And nobody else measured up."

"That's about the size of it."

"What about Andy? I can tell he's crazy about her. Do you think he has a chance?"

"If anybody does, it's Andy. But she's been on her own for… geez, all her life, really. She didn't know her dad and it sounds like her mom was a flake. Out of necessity, she became fiercely independent."

"I admire that about her."

"So do I. Wouldn't want her to be any different." Which was another reason he'd been drawn to Faye from the get-go. Her plans for the future hadn't been based on a wedding, a house and babies.

"By the way, did you find out where the name Josephine came from?"

"Kendall's mother."

"That's sweet. It's a mouthful, though. She'll probably end up Jo or Josie."

"Maybe, but Angie said they intend to call her Jodie. That way they get the Jo part in there for Kendall's mom and the middle initial, or the sound of it, anyway, so my mom's represented, too."

"Cute idea if they can make it stick. Kids take matters into their own hands, though."

"So do adults. Mom started out life as Doris Ann Miller."

"Wow." She laughed. That doesn't fit her at all. I can't picture Doris Ann Miller driving this BPT. When did she change it?"

"I think she began calling herself Desiree early on. Then she made it legal when she turned twenty-one. She revised her middle name to Annabelle and took her last name from her favorite John Wayne character."

"Then she did mean to reference the movie!"

"Yes, ma'am."

"I always wondered about that, but I assumed she was lucky enough to have a cool last name. Turns out she made her own luck."

"That's my mom." Oh, and news flash, he'd made his promise to Faye's mother in front of his own mother. McLintocks didn't break promises.

He had painted himself into a tight and exceedingly ugly corner.

<u>18</u>

Faye walked through the ranch house toward Rowdy Roost holding hands with the cowboy she'd spent the previous evening completely avoiding. Funny how much could change in a mere twenty-four hours.

Gil tugged her back before they pushed through the louvered barroom doors. The celebration had already passed loud and was headed toward deafening. Folks were having a Very Good Time.

He leaned close and even then had to raise his voice to be heard. "You know all the Wenches, right?"

"Not as well as you do, but if they're still color-coded, I doubt I'll mix them up."

"They'll be wearing their colors. They're a little OCD about it. According to them, it's their brand."

"And it works." She'd missed looking into those beautiful blue eyes. Missed it more than she'd ever realized. "Is it just me, or do you feel like last night happened weeks ago?"

"It's not just you. Seems like a couple of months since we were sitting on that quilt in the meadow."

They'd done more than just sit on it. The flicker in his gaze told her he was thinking the same thing. "You know, if time keeps dragging like that, we could live a lifetime in seven days."

His breath caught. "I wouldn't mind."

"Yeah, me, either." Crazy talk. Dangerous talk.

"But I have a sneaky suspicion once we climb into my king-sized bed, we'll look up and it'll be Saturday." Anxiety settled in her chest, making it hard to breathe. He was probably right, but focusing on the end of their story wasn't helpful. "It's wild in there. Think they'd miss us if we turned around and went back out?"

"We're not doing that. And the sooner we make an entrance the sooner we can head for the exit."

"Good point." Still holding her hand, he pushed open the louvered doors.

The Wenches had decorated with balloons, too, using their Wench rainbow colors. Faye spotted each of them moving through the crowd dispensing hugs and food like the fairy godmothers in *Cinderella*.

The combination of the McLintocks and the Wenches equaled a darned good party. Faye had missed so many over the years, some legitimately because of work, but many because of Gil. No more.

Ella spotted them first and hurried over. "I was watching for you. Where are Desiree and Angie?" She was almost shouting.

"Still there," Faye said. "Andy, too."

"What?" Her sister cupped her hand around her ear and leaned toward her.

"Let's go out in the hall."

Ella gave her a thumbs up and led the way back out the louvered doors with Faye and Gil right behind her.

"Desiree's still at the hospital," Faye said once they'd moved far enough to hear each other. "So's Angie."

"Why?" Ella looked worried. "Is everything okay?"

"It's fine. She and Angie are having a hard time leaving."

"Ah. I'm not surprised."

"Andy will drive them back in a little while. Gil and I brought the BPT home."

Ella chuckled. "Picking up the lingo, I see. Before you know it, you'll sound like a Wagon Trainer again."

"C'mon. It's not like I live in a foreign country."

"I know. Just teasing you, sis."

Faye had missed that, too. Missed hanging out with her sister, teasing, fighting, playing the imaginary games she liked and the physical ones Ella was good at. She glanced at Gil. "Would you please get us something to drink?"

"Sure thing. Just tell me what you want."

"Apple cider for me," Ella said.

"Make that two. Thanks, Gil."

"You bet." Giving her hand a squeeze, he let go and walked back into the party.

Ella gazed after him. "He's nuts about you."

"It's mutual." Faye let out a sigh. "Mom said everyone thinks we'll crash and burn. That we can't handle this maneuver. Do you think that?"

"Let's just say I hope you can."

"No matter what, we won't mess up the wedding."

"I know that." Ella's expression softened. "I don't want you to mess up yourself."

"We really don't work as a couple."

"Other than the obvious."

"Other than that. And we're both at the stage of life where we're ready to settle down. But before we do...."

"You want a wild... indulgence."

"Yes."

"I get it. Chemistry like you have with Gil doesn't come along every day."

"I'm aware. On that subject, Gil told me about Desiree and Sky's dad. Do you know that story?"

"I do."

"Maybe that's what I'll have with Gil, minus the secret baby. He'll be my impossible dream."

"And you'll go on to have a bunch of children with different fathers?"

"Hell, no. I might not ever get married, though. I'm not kidding myself. Given a week, Gil could easily ruin me for anyone else."

"Gee, that makes me feel so much better about this." Ella rolled her eyes. "Can't you just commute to UM from here? Penny does."

"Penny teaches English. She has a set schedule. The theater department is a whole other ball of wax. You know the routine. I have to be available nights and weekends, just like you when you're coaching. Could you commute from Missoula to Wagon Train?"

"No."

"See? It's not just a job. It's a way of life."

"Which you love."

"Passionately!"

"More than you love Gil?"

"I don't *love* Gil. I mean I do, as a friend, but this is about a sexual connection. We're not soul mates."

"Liar, liar, pants on fire."

"I admit to the pants on fire part. That much is very true. But I'm not in love with him."

"Because you won't let yourself be?"

"Because there's no point in it, dammit!"

Ella's attention flicked to the louvered doors. "Keep your voice down. He's on his way back with our drinks. Did you deliberately get rid of him?"

"Yeah. I just wanted a chance to talk to you for a minute and find out what you really thought about this. Oh, and let you know I won't screw up the festivities next weekend. Neither will he. That's a pinky-swear promise."

"Like I said, that's not my concern."

Gil showed up with three chilled bottles of apple cider and handed one to each of them.

"Thank you." Faye tapped her bottle against his and Ella's. "To Josephine Desiree."

"Aka Jodie," Ella said.

"A name which may or may not stick," Gil added.

After they'd all taken a sip, he looked at Faye. "Did I take long enough? I can go hang out at the bar for a while if you guys need more time."

Ella smiled. "Spoken like a McLintock. Desiree sure knows how to raise heroes."

"I've noticed that," Faye said. "Gil was the one who turned an embarrassing moment into a choreographed performance this afternoon. I had nuthin'."

"That move was brilliant. I might have taken a video."

Faye gasped. "Of us kissing?"

"Nah. I wouldn't do that. I just filmed the curtain call. I can't promise that nobody filmed the whole thing. You might want to check with Beau. Or Rance."

"Oh, I'll check with them, all right." Gil took a hefty swallow of his cider.

"Is it true you two will be singing Friday night?"

Faye speared him with a look. "Yes, we will."

"Speaking of that, can I sing backup for the *Summer Nights* number?"

Faye nodded. "Absolutely. I'm trying to figure out if we can work out a run-through, maybe Thursday night?"

"I could be available Thursday night. Can Brit sing, too? I'm guessing all my bridesmaids will want to, including her. Except Kendall, of course."

"I'll ask everyone. And we need guys. Would Marsh do it?"

Her sister laughed. "I have no idea." She glanced at Gil. "Would he?"

"Stranger things have happened. Rance is an obvious one, and Beau, of course, our resident ham. Clint, too. Bret — no way. Cheyenne wouldn't, either, even if he didn't have a brand-new baby. I can't say whether Sky or Lucky would."

"Well, that's a good start," Faye said. "I can see Angie wanting to be in on it, and Jess. Tyra, for sure. Gotta rope in the former head cheerleader. Do you think your mom would let us borrow this room for an hour Thursday night?"

"Considering this was her idea, she'll let you have any resources you need."

Ella pulled out her phone. "I'll step into the other room so I can call Brit. I need to anyway to tell her about the baby. See you in a few."

After she left, Gil moved in close. "Are we still planning an early exit?"

"Yes, but I wasn't thinking about this being the perfect time to recruit singers. It is, though."

"Then how about splitting the job? Let me approach my brothers and you talk to the women."

"Good idea. I'm also going to ask Molly and Penny. Penny might not want to. Or be physically able. The way things are going, she might be in labor at the time."

"Let's hope not."

"I hope not, too, for everyone's sake. But Molly might love the idea. And if you're sure Bret's not interested...."

"I can almost guarantee it."

"Then he could watch Zach while she's on stage. And maybe even Maverick if both Jess and

Beau want to sing." Excitement bubbled up inside her. "This is gonna be great."

"You know what? You're right."

"Let's go in." She took a step toward the doorway.

"Wait." He caught her arm. "We haven't discussed sleeping arrangements."

She turned back, her body lighting up as if someone had just plugged her into a socket. "Sleeping arrangements?"

"I'd like you to stay with me. Maybe not the whole week, since you'll need to be at your folks' house Saturday morning to get ready, but at least through Thursday night."

"I...hadn't thought that through."

He smiled. "I haven't thought about much else."

"Neither have I, but I hadn't worked out the logistics."

"Not much to work out. We only have so much time, and my cabin is the only option. Seems silly for you to be driving back and forth."

"It does." Adrenaline shot through her, leaving her shaky.

"In fact, if you want to be packed up by tomorrow around five, I can come get you. Save you some gas."

"And carry me off on your white horse?"

His blue eyes sparkled. "Something like that."

"I'll be ready at five." Maybe by then she'd have figured out how to breathe normally when contemplating the prospect of four long nights in his bed.

<u>19</u>

At last. The reality of driving back to his cabin with Faye in the passenger seat of his truck had been receding for hours like a mirage in the desert. But here they were, pulling away from the ranch house at about the same time they'd left it the night before.

The tension was thick as molasses just like it had been the night before. But it was the good kind of tension that made every word pulse between them like the lazy, sensual beat of a country love song.

She laughed and leaned back against the headrest. "I was so sure *somebody* would have filmed our kiss. But no."

"Not even Beau." In the glow from the dash he traced the curve of her throat, imagined kissing her there, sliding his hand up under her shirt....

"Because it would have been creepy. And they like us too much to do something creepy."

"Yeah." He reached for her hand, needing to touch her. "They do. They may think our plan is doomed, but we have their support no matter how it goes." He wove his fingers through hers. So soft.

Did she mind that his weren't? "Beau took me aside and asked if I needed fresh condoms."

"*Fresh* condoms?"

"He just bought some. I guess that qualifies as fresh." He was making her smile. That little dent in her cheek was another place he wanted to kiss.

"Why does he need them? I thought they were planning to have another kid."

"They were. He'd finally come around, believed he could handle putting Jess through it again. Then last week he learned that a baby might end up facing the wrong way, which was potentially dangerous. Now he's back to thinking one kid is good enough." The topic of kids hit a tender spot in his chest. He'd have to toughen up on that subject, at least for this week.

"Beau's a good guy."

"Yeah."

"Your whole family is wonderful. I was an idiot to cut myself off the way I did. We need to make a pact that we'll stay friends."

"We don't need a pact. I plan to be your friend for the rest of my life." No matter what it took.

"What if they're right and it's really tough to end things?"

"Doesn't matter how tough it is. I'm prepared for it to be difficult. I choose to have these few days — more like these few nights — and pay whatever price is required." And pretend that it wasn't killing him when she left for Missoula.

Her fingers tightened around his. "Ella had it right. Desiree knows how to raise heroes."

"I appreciate that, but I probably need to turn the discussion around one more time. I'm willing to accept the consequences, but are you?"

"I think so."

"Are you sure? You just said *what if they're right* like you believe they're wrong and we'll be fine with letting go at the end of the week."

"I like to think positive."

"And that's generally a good thing." He pulled up next to her car. No puddles tonight. "But before we go inside, maybe you should picture being miserable for a while and decide how you feel about putting yourself through it. Could be a few days, could be a few weeks, could be—"

"Is that what you've done?"

"As a matter of fact."

"You've projected the possibility that you'll be miserable for weeks, maybe even months?"

"I have. I've imagined my worst-case scenario in vivid detail, complete with the possibility of drinking 'til I puke."

She made a face. "And you still want to go through with this?"

"Yep."

"I can't say that I've done that. Definitely not the drinking 'til I puke." She peered at him. "Is that really something you might do?"

"Probably not. But it's on the list."

"Not on mine. When I'm miserable I binge-watch old Westerns and eat Oreos."

"Why Oreos?"

"There's something soothing about twisting them apart and licking the filling."

"Uh, okay." Something sexy about it, too. Licking factored into his plans for tonight. He unlatched his seatbelt as his jeans began to pinch. If he'd kept his mouth shut on this topic, they wouldn't still be sitting in the truck. But he was worried she'd glossed over the train-wreck potential of their adventure.

"All right, I'm picturing days, maybe weeks of Hoss Cartwright and Little Joe while my apartment fills up with empty Oreo packages." She shuddered. "Happy, now?"

"Of course not. I just—"

"Oh, and tonight I told Ella there's a chance you'll ruin me for every other guy. Does that count as worst-case scenario thinking?"

"It counts, but it's highly unlikely." She'd ruined him for other women, though. He hadn't known that until he'd kissed her again. Once he'd touched down on that velvet mouth, he'd understood what had been missing from every relationship he'd had in the past ten years. Magic.

She unlatched her seatbelt and turned to him, a cute smile on those sassy lips. "What if we've built up our expectations and the reality turns out to be ordinary, garden-variety sex? If we're talking negativity, that's a possibility, too."

He grinned, the knot of anxiety in his chest loosening. "No, it's not."

A challenge gleamed in her gray eyes. "You don't know that."

"Yes, I do." The ache in his groin wouldn't be satisfied with ordinary.

"Prove it."

"Yes, ma'am." He reached for the door. "Stay put. I'm coming for you."

He gasped as he climbed out and his zipper jabbed him in the crotch. The opening move he had in mind might not end up being as graceful as he'd pictured, but he had one shot at a dramatic beginning and he wasn't about to blow it.

She'd thrown down the gauntlet, all right. Ordinary, garden-variety sex? Not on his watch.

He hobbled around the truck, cussing under his breath and visualizing the Sapphires to depressurize. He didn't need to be hard as an anvil now. When the time was right, he'd have no trouble rising to the occasion.

The passenger door stood open, but she'd stayed put as he'd requested. She'd swiveled to face him, though. "Did your mom teach you to help ladies out of trucks?"

"She did." He gazed at her and concentrated on controlling his reaction so he'd be able to walk without pain. "She warned us that some women might consider it patronizing, so we'd need to adjust our behavior accordingly."

"Patronizing women isn't your style. Helping women out of vehicles is old-fashioned, but in your case, it fits."

"You think of me as old-fashioned? Doesn't sound like a compliment."

"It is, though. When you offer your hand to help me in and out of a truck, I view it as a gesture of respect. Makes me feel special."

"Good, because—"

"Also gets me hot."

His breath hitched. Better get this show on the road before he exploded. "Then allow me." He held out his hand.

She slipped her silky palm over his, curled her fingers and started down, holding his gaze.

His heart played leapfrog in his chest as he waited for her to put both feet on the ground. The moment she did, he released his grip and scooped her up in his arms.

She squealed. "You're gonna *carry* me in there?"

"I am." He nudged the door shut with his hip and settled her more firmly against his chest. "Any objections?" He headed toward the steps.

"Are you kidding? This is *awesome.*" She grabbed him around the neck. "I've always wanted to be carried to bed. I hope you lifted from your knees, though. I'd hate for you to strain your—"

"Shush." Pausing, he gave her a quick kiss. "I've got this."

She sighed and nestled against him. "Am I too heavy?"

"No." As he mounted the steps his breathing roughened.

"Then why are you breathing hard?"

"Anticipation."

"Oh. I get that." She sounded breathy, too. "I have a request."

"Name it."

"Can we skip foreplay?"

He choked out a laugh. "I think this is the foreplay."

"Yes! Just carry me in there and toss me on the bed. That's my fantasy."

"Toss you? So you bounce?" He paused in front of the door. Could he hold on and still reach the knob? Maybe not.

"Well, maybe not quite that—"

"Can you get the doorknob? Please?"

"You betcha." Holding him around the neck with one hand, she turned the knob and gave the door a little push.

"That's good." He shouldered his way into the house and kicked the door shut.

"It's dark in here."

"Yep." Seemed fitting. The woods had been dark, too. "It's okay. I know where I'm going." Did she remember he'd said the same thing that night?

"I should hope so."

His breath caught. "You said that when we—"

"I know. Then I said *my heart's doing the Indy 500* and you said—"

"Mine, too."

"Here's one I didn't say. My panties are wet."

He clenched his jaw. "We're definitely skipping foreplay."

"I'll take off my clothes while you put on the condom."

"Good plan." He walked into his bedroom, faintly lit by a soft nightlight in the bathroom and a silvery glow through the window courtesy of the stars and a crescent moon. "And I'm not tossing you."

"You're sure?"

"I'm sure." He laid her down on the quilt. "Because I have to do this one thing." Lowering his head, he kissed her, losing himself in the wonder of it for a few seconds before his body's demands forced him to pull back and begin wrenching off his clothes.

"You *had* to stop and kiss me?"
"Yes, ma'am."
"Why?"
"Magic."

<u>20</u>

Magic. Such a glittery word for the earthy, desperate urges driving Faye as she toed off her boots and tore off her shirt and jeans. Gil's ragged breathing and soft curses as he wrestled with his boots spoke more of unbridled lust than magic.

A bathroom nightlight and a faint sparkle of stars and a crescent moon gave her a shadowy view, enough to see that he yanked off his shirt while it was still half buttoned and fumbled with his belt buckle, eagerness making him clumsy. The floor was soon littered with his clothes and hers.

She finished first, threw back the covers and stretched out on the cool sheets, quivering and achy. "Hurry."

"Almost there." He grabbed a condom from the bedside table drawer and ripped open the packet.

"Wait!" She sat up and reached for the lamp switch. "You promised I'd get a chance to see—"

"Not now." He climbed in, his chest brushing the tips of her breasts, his thighs sliding against hers. "The dark feels right." An intimate touch, a firm thrust, and he was deep inside, his big body trembling. "Damn." The whispered word was more of a prayer than a curse.

"Mm." Arms tightening around him, she took a shaky breath. There it was, the perfect connection. She hadn't imagined it all those years ago. Hadn't appreciated how rare it was.

He pushed a little deeper. The muted click of total engagement was only in her head. The warm flow of air when he sighed — that was real.

His face was in shadow except for his beautiful eyes, which reflected... starlight. *Magic.*

"I remember," he murmured.

"Mm-hm."

"But then I came." His chest heaved. "Not this time." He eased back. "I promise. Not this time."

She held her breath and concentrated on the delicious friction as he glided back in, setting off tiny explosions along the way. When he tucked himself in and paused, she gradually released the air in her lungs. The press of his cock brought an answering ripple from her core. A prelude.

He remained still, panting a little. "Need to go slow for now."

His husky voice was the sexiest sound she'd ever heard. Clearly he was on the edge. Just as clearly it took everything he had to hold back. And he was doing it. For her.

He wouldn't have to hold back much longer. She pressed her fingertips into the bunched muscles of his broad back. "I'm..." She had to stop and clear her throat. "I'm close."

"I know." He gulped. "I feel it. Drives me... crazy."

"Sorry."

"Don't be. It's what... I'm after." He drew back and rocked forward again. "I want to feel you come. Feel it when I'm locked in tight."

Another tremor. Stronger this time.

His breath hissed through his clenched teeth. "That's it. Let go."

As if she had a choice. She erupted with a keening cry, arching into him, tossing her head from side-to-side. He bore down, absorbing the shock waves, gulping for air.

When the undulations tapered off, he began to move. Something had changed. His breathing had evened out. His strokes were easy, unhurried.

Yet moments ago, he'd been ready to explode. Breathless and trembling, she looked into his starlit eyes. "Gil?"

"Second wind." His gaze locked with hers. "Having fun?"

"Big fun." She swallowed, her body humming with pleasure as his steady thrusts and the intensity in his eyes built the tension all over again. "But... how did you—"

"Tell you later." He picked up the pace. "Busy right now."

She gasped as her core tightened. "Don't let me... interrupt."

"Don't think you could." His voice grew hoarse as he pumped faster. "Come for me, Faye. *Come for me.*"

She did, loudly. So did he, with a triumphant yell as he buried himself in her quaking body and shuddered in the grip of his climax.

For several seconds he stayed braced above her, his breathing harsh. At last, with a deep groan, he laid his cheek on her shoulder and sank down, lightly resting on her sweat-slicked body but not giving her his whole weight.

She ran her fingers through his damp hair. "Relax. You won't squish me."

"I might."

"You didn't the last time."

"I'm quite a few pounds heavier than I was then." He snuggled closer. "But since you're inviting me, I'll chance squishing you a little bit."

"You do feel different from last time. I guess it's all that muscle from swinging hammers."

"You feel different, too."

"Are you referring to my chest measurements?"

"Um, not exactly."

"Sure you are. It's okay. I know I wasn't very busty back then. I was jealous of the girls who were. I saw you looking at them."

"As we've established, I was eighteen and stupid. Yeah, I looked, and appreciated, but they didn't affect me the way you did."

"You're just being nice."

"I'm telling it like it is. Or was. Maybe you didn't fill out your bikini top as spectacularly as they did on Senior Ditch Day. But you gave me the worst case of blue balls I've ever had."

She smiled. "I sure wish I'd known *that.*"

"Well, now you do. And I need to take care of this condom. Be right back. Don't go away."

"I couldn't if I wanted to. You melted all my bones."

"That's what I like to hear." He chuckled and headed for the bathroom. On his way in, he called out *tell me more.*

That was her cue. Sitting up, she sang it back to him. Would he sing for her?

When he belted an answering lyric from *Summer Nights*, she grinned. "You faker! There's nothing wrong with your voice!"

"That's nice to hear. I'm not a good judge."

"I think you've been singing more than you let on."

"I have, but only when I'm alone."

"Why?"

"Maybe it's silly, but I worry that Bret—"

"You need to talk to him about it."

"You're right. I will. Before the rehearsal dinner"

"Your voice is a gift. Something to share."

"I hadn't thought of it like that."

"Well, please do. It's lovely. In fact, you have more resonance now that your chest is bigger."

"Does that mean you have more resonance?"

"Yes, I do, smarty pants."

He came out of the bathroom, his broad shoulders and lean hips subtly backlit by the soft glow behind him. "Will you sing for me?"

"I just did."

"A whole song."

He didn't have to say which one. "Now?"

"If you're willing. I've missed hearing you sing it and... it would be... I don't know... nice."

"But it's out of order. Last time I sang to you before we had sex."

"Which was the main reason we had sex."

"Really? You just said you had blue balls all day."

"I also was scared to death that I'd make a fool of myself because you knew how and I didn't. I'd pretty much given up on making that move. But then you sang to me, and I decided it was worth making a fool of myself."

"Was it?"

He approached the bed. "A week ago I would have said no, but now I can say yes. That night brought us to this night." He sat on the edge of the bed, reached for her hand, wove his fingers through hers. "I love that song."

Warmth filled her chest. She used to love singing for him, with him. She'd latched onto the idea of a public performance for the rehearsal dinner for that very reason. Why shouldn't it also be part of this private time they'd carved out for themselves?

Pulling air deep into her lungs, she began the song that would forever be tied to Gil McLintock.

21

Hopelessly Devoted to You. Just words in a song, not a declaration of Faye's undying love. Gil didn't care. He'd take those words into his heart because he needed every last one.

Sure, they were a lie, but for this week, he'd believe the lie. He'd act as if she was hopelessly devoted to him when in fact it was the other way around.

He'd ducked the truth for ten long years but here it was, smacking him in the face. He loved Faye and she loved her job. It would claim her once the week ended. In the meantime, she was here, singing to him as if the words came straight from her heart.

For this moment, they probably did. He occupied a place there, probably always would. Did he crave more real estate? Yes, he did. Would he try to expand his holdings? Not a chance.

But he'd always have this — sitting naked on his bed with Faye singing him a love song. He'd store the memory with the others. In the next few days he'd create more, a mental scrapbook.

She kept her gaze on him as she sang, but he couldn't read her expression in the dim light. She likely couldn't read his, either, which was a blessing. Adoration had to be written all over his face.

She kept the volume down just as she had in the woods, even the parts that called for a full-throttle delivery when she'd performed them for more than an audience of one. While he thrilled to her powerful voice when it rattled the rafters, this quiet, intimate version was his favorite, maybe because no one had heard it but him.

Singing it that night years ago had been his idea, and she hadn't wanted to, saying it was too loud and might scare the critters who were out and about.

Then don't sing it loud, he'd said, clueless that this version would burrow deep into his chest and steal his heart. She'd had it ever since.

Any hope that he'd moved on had vanished last night. This moment, one he'd chosen, permanently sealed his fate. He would never be over Faye. And that was fine with him.

When she finished, his throat was tight. He had to clear it twice. "Thank you."

"It's your song, you know."

"It is?" He hoped to hell she hadn't made the leap and guessed he was the one who was hopelessly devoted. "How so?"

"All these years, I couldn't hear it without thinking of you."

"And cursing my name?"

"I've never cursed your name. Sometimes the song would make me sad, but then I'd remember all those wonderful rehearsal kisses. You sure didn't kiss like a virgin."

"Neither did you. And FYI, that's your song. I can't hear it without thinking of you."

"Then maybe it's *our* song."

"Maybe it is." By some miracle he kept his voice steady, as if the phrase *our song* hadn't been a surprisingly sharp punch to the gut. But he quickly rallied. Just because they'd end their intimate relationship at the end of the week didn't mean they couldn't have a special song.

She gave his hand a squeeze. "Is it time to turn on the light?"

"We could, but I'm liking the nostalgia of this unplanned darkness. It adds to the do-over theme. On the other hand, if you're ready to light up the place, then—"

"Let's keep the lights off, at least for tonight. Tomorrow's soon enough for me to satisfy my curiosity about your manly attributes."

"You don't have to wait until tomorrow." He drew their clasped hands into his lap. "There's another way to find out what you want to know." He slipped his hand free. "Could be a lot more fun, too."

She laughed and began to explore, her warm fingers on his cock making him shiver. "Why yes, it certainly could. And the verdict is — you were robbed of your foreskin at a tender age."

"Which means sex isn't supposed to be as good?"

"So they say." She wrapped her fingers around his increasingly hard cock.

He dragged in a breath. "If it got any better than what we just had, I'd be a dead man."

"Seemed like you had a good time." She squeezed gently.

"Seems like I'm ready to have another one. But I don't want to be pushy. If you'd like to take a break, grab something to drink, maybe a sna..." He lost track of what he'd meant to say as she continued to fondle him.

"I have what I want right here." She held onto his pride and joy while reaching for the bedside table drawer with her free hand. "It's just missing its party outfit."

"Mm." Combine her nimble fingers with her take-charge attitude and his vocabulary deserted him. Also the ability to breathe like a normal person.

After plucking a condom packet from the drawer, she nudged it closed and tried to open the wrapper with her teeth. It didn't want to cooperate.

He found his voice. "Need help?"

"This is supposed to work." She tried again. "To hell with it." Releasing his cock, she used both hands and ripped open the packet. "It would be a handy trick if it worked."

"It does."

"You can do it?" She pulled out the condom and began rolling it on.

"Yeah." That was all he had the time or the breath to say. He was too busy focusing on his control mechanism. Wouldn't do to come while she was suiting him up.

"There you go. Lie down, please. This'll be my show."

"Yes, ma'am." He stretched out on his back and she wasted no time straddling him, her hands braced on either side of his chest.

The light was dim, but not so dim that it robbed him of the erotic visual. Her sexy pose made his groin throb and his cock feel like a rocket poised on a launchpad.

She ducked her head, her hair swinging down to tickle his chest while she gauged her position. Balancing on one hand, she clutched his hard-as-iron bad boy, probably to facilitate the connection.

He couldn't see much in the dark, especially with her hair dangling in front of his eyes. He squeezed them shut anyway, along with every other muscle in his body, including the ones that would keep him from coming.

Her breathing was almost as ragged as his. He took comfort in that. He wasn't the only super-excited participant in this bed. She'd had two orgasms, but that didn't stop her from wanting another one.

She took him in slowly and he told himself sad stories all the way down to keep from exploding on contact. How long before his hair-trigger response would mellow? He'd likely need more than a week.

Her silky tush brushed his thighs as his cock nudged the entrance to her womb. His lungs pushed out a sigh as if his body recognized a perfect fit.

She lifted her head to gaze at him. "This is good." Her voice had the low, sultry tone of a woman getting what she needed from the man between her thighs.

His heart thudded in his chest, shaking his whole body. "Uh-huh."

"Not garden variety."

"No."

"Thank you, Gil."

"Anytime."

She began to move.

He stayed still, curled his hands into fists and gulped for air as she drove him straight out of his mind. He wanted to watch. Had to close his eyes or risk losing it. The darkness didn't completely disguise the seductive movement of her breasts and hips.

But the lack of the visual amplified the sounds, the liquid rhythm, picking up speed, her gasps mingling with his, a whimper, his groan, then his plea... *slow down.*

"Can't!" Instead she went faster, crying out, taking him with her.

With a roar of surrender, he grabbed her hips, surged upward and came hard, his muscles clenched as the spasms carried him to a place of vibrant colors and rich, undulating textures, a place that belonged to Faye, only Faye.

He might have called her name. It echoed in his head, over and over. Probably had said it. Dazed, he gradually relaxed onto the mattress, his eyes still squeezed shut.

Her lips touched his, a tender kiss that made his heart stutter. "Turn me loose," she murmured.

Sure enough, his hands were welded to her hips. He pried his fingers away from her soft skin. If he'd left bruises he'd never forgive himself. "Hope I didn't hurt—"

"No way." She kissed him again, gently climbed off her perch and stretched out beside him. "I loved how you grabbed me."

The huskiness in her voice stroked his still vibrating nerves, sending aftershocks through his system. His chest heaved. "Couldn't help myself."

"I know. That's what made it so exciting."

He didn't want to move. Had to, though. This position didn't lend itself to loitering. Anchoring the condom, he rolled to his side and got out of bed. Staggered once.

"Want me to—"

"I've got this." He took a breath. "You pack a punch, lady."

"So do you, cowboy."

Warmth filled his chest. Finally, after royally screwing up what could have been a sweet teenage romance, he'd been given a chance to make amends. For that, he'd be eternally grateful.

<u>22</u>

Lying on her side facing the open door of the bathroom, Faye watched the shifting light and listened to the water going on and off as Gil took care of business. "Condoms are a pain, aren't they?"

"I guess. But I'm glad they exist."

"Me, too. But I'll bet it's more fun without them."

"Like I said before, this might be as much fun as I can handle. You got me so good I almost couldn't walk."

"I don't usually have that effect."

"Yeah, well I don't usually get affected like this, either. Evidently we're a combustible combo."

"And we almost didn't find that out."

"Almost." He walked toward her, clearly steadier than when he'd gone in. "So what now? Are you thirsty? Hungry?"

"Sleepy." She yawned. "It's been a big day."

"Has it? I didn't notice."

"Business as usual? Just another day at Rowdy Ranch?"

"Pretty much." He crossed to the bed and slid in beside her. "Until now."

"Got something up your sleeve? Oh, wait, you don't have sleeves."

"Sure don't." He gathered her close. "Never did care for pajamas. Once I left Mom's house I ditched 'em for good."

"So going to bed starkers is normal?"

"Yes, ma'am." He nestled her head against his shoulder. "Ready to get some shuteye?"

"Not until you tell me what's happening right now that's different."

"You. Lying in my bed."

"Well, that's obviously different, but not hugely different. I'm sure I'm not the first to—"

"Actually, you are."

She lifted her head so fast she clipped his jaw. "Sorry!" She touched the spot, "Did that hurt?"

"I'm fine. What about your head?"

"I have a hard head. In more ways than one."

He chuckled. "I'd go along with that."

"What do you mean, I'm the first one in this bed? Did you just buy it? Or change the mattress? Because I don't think switching the mattress counts, but if you just bought the—"

"This is the bed I got when I moved in. Mattress, too, for that matter."

Propping herself on her elbow, she peered down at him. "I can't see your face very well, so I can't tell if you're teasing."

"Not teasing. I've never shared this bed with anyone until now."

"That can't be true."

"You really are a hard-headed woman." Laughter rippled in his voice. "Trust me, it's true.

Let me know if I snore. If I do, maybe the good sex will make up for it."

"But you had condoms stashed in the bedside table drawer! That's a dead giveaway."

"What if I put them there this morning?"

Her breath hitched. "That's not normally where they are?"

"I keep a supply under the sink in the bathroom. The extras are still there. Go look if you don't believe me."

"I believe you." She swallowed. "I'm just... surprised that you've never brought someone out here before."

"Maybe not so surprising. It's a drive, and my girlfriends have always lived in town. It's mostly a convenience issue."

"But with me, you had no choice." Her ego deflated a little.

He cupped her cheek. "I guess you could look at it that way, but I look at it as closing the circle."

"What circle?"

"Think about it." He stroked his thumb slowly back and forth. "You were my first, and now you're the first one sharing this bed with me. That seems right."

Her chest grew warm and squishy. "It does." What a beautiful concept. And yet... "You could be creating a problem for yourself, though. If you give this bed sentimental value, what will you do about it... later on?" She couldn't bring herself to say *after I'm gone.*

He shrugged. "I'll just get a new bed."

"No! That's ridiculous!"

"Yeah, it is." He pulled her close and kissed her in that same tender way he had earlier. "New sheets, though. Definitely new sheets."

"That's more like it." But she didn't believe new sheets would do the trick and he likely didn't, either. He'd end up tossing the bed.

_23_

Gil overslept, something he hadn't done in years. His internal clock had become so reliable he'd stopped setting an alarm. Good thing Bret called.

His brother's ringtone woke him, but he had to search under the clothes still lying on the floor to locate his phone. "Hey, bro."

"Hey, lover boy. Hope I didn't interrupt anything."

"No, no." Gil scrubbed a hand over his face and glanced toward the bed where a beautifully tousled Faye was blinking at him. "It's fine."

"Glad to hear it. I called because I had a hunch you might forget we're supposed to drive to Missoula this morning."

"We are?" Then his brain kicked into gear. "Yes, we are. We volunteered to pick up the groomsmen outfits."

"And check out the sale on a snazzy new torch you're excited about. Or were. It might have moved down on your list."

"No, I still want to take a look." He paused. "Remind me again when we planned to leave?"

"In about thirty minutes. Which should give us time to get back and open the shop at one, like we posted."

"Right. Absolutely. Um... did we decide who was driving?"

Bret cracked up. "Me, obviously. You sound wasted. Can you make it in thirty minutes? Or do you want to bail? I can pick up the outfits and we can just forget about the—"

"I'll be ready in thirty." He squinted at his phone. Yeah, he'd *way* overslept. "See you then."

"Alrighty! Can't wait to hear how things are going." He was still laughing as he disconnected.

"I need to get out of here." Faye sat up and the covers fell away from her breasts — her lovely, soft, touchable breasts.

He groaned. "I should've told Bret I couldn't—"

"Nope. Mom, Brit, Ella and I have a mani-pedi appointment at ten." She climbed out of bed and rummaged through the clothes on the floor. "If I leave in the next fifteen minutes, I'll have time to get myself together."

Like the besotted idiot he was, he stood like a statue, mesmerized by her limber, graceful movements. They hadn't just sung together ten years ago, they'd danced.

She snatched up the last of her clothes and started toward the bedroom door.

"Where are you going?"

"Down to your guest bathroom."

"You can have mine."

She paused in the doorway, her gray eyes filled with laughter, her smile warm. "You need it. All your stuff's there and you have to shave and shower. I just need to freshen up and get dressed."

"Oh." She was thinking and he was not. "Okay. I'll shave first, so don't leave without saying goodbye."

"I won't." She dashed down the hall, the patter of her bare feet on the wood floor the cutest sound ever. No one had ever run barefoot on his floors, not even him.

Someone could, though, without worrying about splinters. He'd made sure the floors were finished right when he had them put in, and Angie had helped him maintain them.

"You'll probably have kids running around barefoot someday," his sister had said.

Her prediction hadn't come true so far, and he couldn't picture it happening any time soon. He hadn't met the woman he'd want to have kids with. Well, he had, but....

Sighing, he walked into the bathroom, took the can of shaving cream out of the mirrored cabinet and lathered up. This wasn't the most optimal morning after, but he'd do better tomorrow.

For starters, he'd take a look at his calendar for the week and then find out what she had scheduled. He and Bret juggled their farrier appointments with time in the shop so at least one of them was there on weekdays. Just not this morning since they had errands in Missoula.

They could get away with closing for half a day now and then in a town the size of Wagon

Train. Most everyone knew it was only the two of them running the shop plus the farrier business. Folks made allowances.

He was one razor stroke away from finishing his shave when the tick, tick, tick of her boot heels told him she was dressed and ready to head out. His stomach lurched. He didn't want her to leave.

And that was a bad sign. He scraped off the last of the shaving cream and grabbed a hand towel to mop his face. When he lowered the towel, she appeared in the mirror.

She looked… not sad, exactly, but…wistful? Like maybe she didn't want to leave any more than he wanted her to.

Tossing the towel on the counter, he turned around. "I wish you didn't have to go."

"I wish I didn't, either." She stepped toward him and cupped his freshly shaven face. "You smell nice."

He pulled her close. "So do you."

"Liar. I did the best I could with a little soap and water, but I desperately need a shower."

"So you say." He splayed his fingers over her denim-covered tush and squeezed.

Heat flashed in her gray eyes. "I haven't had one since yesterday." She slid her palms up his chest.

"Me, either. And if we didn't have to go anywhere, I'd talk you into waiting a while longer. Nothing like the smell of good sex first thing in the morning. Beats coffee any day."

Her breath caught. "Are you suggesting we change things up tomorrow?"

"Strongly suggesting. Assuming we can coordinate our calendars."

"It's an excellent goal." She swallowed and backed away. "I'm leaving so we can honor the obligations we made before we knew...."

"How great it would be?"

She nodded. Then she fished in her pocket and pulled out his class ring. "Just so you know, I haven't lost it."

"To be honest, I haven't given that ring another thought."

"Well, I have, and I'm glad you gave it to me." She shoved it back in her pocket. "Bye." She turned and hurried toward the bedroom door.

"Five o'clock?"

"On the dot!" She walked faster. "Don't be late!"

He snorted. Like that was even a remote possibility.

Once she was out the door, he forced himself to stop thinking about her. Otherwise he wouldn't be ready when Bret showed up. The guy was notoriously prompt.

He powered through his morning routine. A cup of black coffee and peanut butter toast was breakfast. While he munched the toast and swigged the coffee, he scrolled through his appointments for the week.

He'd accepted only three shoeing jobs in case Marsh or his mom needed him for wedding-related stuff. As the oldest of the unattached males in the family, he was tapped more often than Lucky or Rance. Lucky was reliable, but running the bookstore didn't give him much flexibility. And

Rance... well, he was doing better, but he was still easily distracted and not great with details.

Bret pulled up outside as he drained the last of his coffee. Shoving his wallet in his back pocket, he picked up his phone and headed out the door.

No doubt about it, the deep blue of Bret's truck was a crowd pleaser. As he walked toward it, he almost wished he'd chosen a flashier color. But the magnetic McLintock Metalworks signs stood out way better on tan and advertising the business was important.

Still, Faye would likely think Bret's truck was prettier. Not that it mattered. She'd only be riding in his tan one a few times this week. After that....

He shut down that line of thinking real quick. There be dragons, as the old maps used to say.

He climbed into Bret's truck and found an insulated travel mug in the cup holder. "Is that for me?"

"Figured you wouldn't have time for your usual two cups."

"Thanks. You figured right."

He backed the truck around and pulled out. "Also thought you might need the caffeine to stay awake."

"For your information, I got almost eight hours of sleep." He picked up the mug.

"Good Lord! Was the sex that bad?"

"The sex was incredible. But we'd both had a long day and so we slept." Twisting the top of the mug, he sipped the hot brew.

"You do know you sound like you're married, right?"

"Is that how married people talk?"

"It's not the words so much as the sensible behavior. You have fun sex and then you go to sleep, because staying up all night having more sex is stupid when you have a whole lifetime of sharing a bed. While you, on the other hand, are supposed to be making every minute count because the clock is ticking."

"Thanks for reminding me."

"Clearly you need to be reminded. I thought you were going into this with your eyes wide open, which is the only way you're going to survive it."

"Just because I know what the ending will be doesn't mean I have to focus on it twenty-four-seven."

"I guess that's true. I just don't want you to start thinking something will change, because I don't see that happening."

"Neither do I."

"Good." Bret drove in silence for a while. "You don't have to tell me if you don't want to. You don't ever have to tell me. But if you were thinking of eventually explaining what happened ten years ago, now would be a logical time."

"It's not a pretty story."

"I already know that much. But judging from the way she defended you when you were heaping blame on yourself yesterday, I'm guessing it's a forgivable offense."

"Maybe, maybe not. I would have told you back then, but we promised each other we'd never say anything to anyone."

"Are you still bound by that?"

"No. In fact, she'll probably tell Ella the next chance she gets. Maybe her mom, too."

"You gonna tell ours?"

"Depends. But I will tell you."

Bret glanced at him. "You two had sex, didn't you?"

"If you can call it that."

"So really bad sex. Was she a virgin?"

"Yes." He hesitated. "And so was I. I lasted about three seconds."

Bret's lips twitched. Then a snort escaped. "Sorry. It's just—"

"Go ahead and laugh. That part's funny as hell."

"You were always so sure of yourself. I figured my little brother had done the deed before I even made it to first base."

"Nope."

"I mean, seriously, you were Danny Zuco. Nothing cooler than that. Naturally you'd sail through your first time while the rest of us made a complete ass of ourselves. This is comforting. Very comforting."

"Yeah, well, I was more of an ass than any of you. My sad performance was bad enough, but then I didn't reach out the next day, or the next, or… ever."

"Okay, that stinks."

"I also didn't tell her it was my first time. I let her think it was because I'd had too much to drink. In her mind, I had sex with her and then I dumped her."

"Which is exactly what you did."

"Only because I was so humiliated and embarrassed that I couldn't face her. She knows that now."

"But she didn't know it then! And she'd also promised not to tell so she couldn't even cry on someone's shoulder."

"Right."

"And she's still willing to have sex with you? She hasn't tried to cut out your heart with a rusty knife?"

"Not yet. That part may come later."

<u>**24**</u>

Faye couldn't remember the last time she'd had a mani-pedi day with her mom and her sister. Brit was almost a member of the family, so having her along made a cozy foursome.

Ella chose the shade of polish, teal and pearly white to match her wedding colors. She'd picked the same ones a year ago when she'd almost married a dirty rotten cheater. She still loved the color combo and had decided not to let that nasty experience influence her, especially since Faye and Brit had kept their teal dresses.

Lunch at the Buffalo followed the mani-pedi session, which gave Faye a chance to consult with Tyra about Friday night's *Grease* number.

Bringing over a glass of iced tea for herself, Tyra pulled up a chair and sat with them while they had lunch. "I've been thinking about this ever since you asked me last night. It'll be fun no matter what, but if we had costumes...."

"That would definitely ramp up the excitement." Ella glanced at Faye. "Any chance Mrs. Allred kept the ones from when you guys did it?"

"There's an excellent chance. Drama departments keep anything that's still usable and not a pain to store."

"Then—"

"Are you sure you want to mess with costumes, though?" Faye's years of experience kicked in. "If they belong to the school, we'd have to be super careful with them. We couldn't wear them all night and risk spilling on them."

"I'm game to do the quick-change thing." Brit turned to Ella. "But it's your rehearsal dinner, literally your show. And your call."

"I'm all for it if we can borrow the costumes. The bathroom's kinda small, but—"

"There's the office," Tyra said.

"Exactly. Like we did when I had to get out of my godawful wedding dress last year. We could fit three people in there, maybe four. So I say let's go for it, Faye. I've always wanted to wear a poodle skirt and crinolines."

"It's not as much fun as you imagine. You turn into a Saint Bernard with a waggy tail. You can clear knickknacks off a coffee table in no time."

"Then we'd need to see how they work prior to Friday," Tyra said.

"I'll get with Mrs. Allred as soon as possible, maybe even today if she's around."

"She likely will be. Everybody's prepping for first semester." Ella pretended to admire her new manicure. "Except me, because I'm D-O-N-E."

"Then I'll contact her once we leave here." This project was becoming more complicated than she'd intended.

If she borrowed the costumes, she'd be responsible for their safety and transportation. Ordinarily she wouldn't mind, except every minute spent messing with them was a minute stolen from her time with Gil. She had only herself to blame, though. She'd jumped on the idea when Desiree had suggested it yesterday.

"You're frowning," Ella said. "Would you rather not get into the costume thing? Is it too much trouble?"

She met her sister's worried gaze, her sister who'd always wanted to wear a poodle skirt and whose wedding was only days away. This week was about her, not Gil McLintock. "I was just working out the logistics. We should definitely try to borrow costumes. It'll be so much cooler with poodle skirts."

"Or tight black pants with red heels," Brit said. "I'm going with that look. I might be able to put something together without raiding the drama department's costume shop."

"I was just thinking that." Tyra pushed back her chair. "If I can organize my own costume then I can wear it all night. And less for you to wrangle, Faye."

"Don't worry about that. I'm happy to do it. I'll alert Gil. He can find out if the guys are on board with the costume thing."

Tyra laughed. "Clint will be. Putting on a black leather jacket and tight jeans? He'll be all over that. So will Rance. And Beau. Oh, my God, you'll have to reel him in or he'll steal the show."

"He can try." Faye had experienced what happened to Gil when he slipped into his Danny role. Beau didn't stand a chance.

After lunch she checked out the sound system with Tyra and paced off the dimensions of the stage. Standing on it, her resistance to the work involved evaporated.

She lived for this kind of thing. And bonus, she'd get to perform with Gil in a planned and rehearsed number, not some lame impromptu bit at the reunion.

No one had brought up their *indulgence* during the mani-pedi session or at lunch. She appreciated that. The focus had stayed where it was supposed to — on the rehearsal dinner and the wedding.

On the drive back to her mom's house, she sat in the back of her mom's SUV with Brit and texted Mrs. Allred, who responded immediately. After a quick back-and-forth, Faye ended the thread with a thumbs-up emoji. "Hey, guys, Mrs. Allred can meet me at the school at two-thirty. She still has some costumes from the show. We're in business."

"Woo-hoo!" Ella, turned around from the front passenger seat and high-fived both of them. "I'll go, too, if that's okay."

"Of course."

"I'd go if I could," Brit said. "But I promised my boss I'd be back at two."

"No worries." Faye patted her knee. "Are you sure you don't want a poodle skirt? I didn't mean to scare you with the Saint Bernard image."

"You didn't scare me, but I can picture it. I'm surprised Ella wants one after her disaster of a wedding dress last year. Talk about a ginormous skirt."

"It was also long, which made it a tripping hazard," Ella said. "And I had to wear that iron maiden thing under it. I'm so much happier with the dress I have this year."

"It's breathtaking." Faye had been able to participate in the hunt for a wedding dress because Ella had shopped for it in Missoula.

"I love it, too, and Brit has a point. I might regret the poodle skirt. But you have to wear one. That's iconic. And the blonde wig, if they kept it."

"We'll see what they saved." She wanted the wig, too. And the other one with all the curls. And the black skin-tight outfit from *You're the One That I Want.* Her bust size had changed, but the rest of her hadn't. If luck was with her, all her costumes for the show were still there. And she just might use them.

After they reached the house and said goodbye to Brit, Ella suggested taking her truck over to Wagon Train High. Faye was grateful. Depending on the haul, they might need more room than her little sedan could give them.

The minute they pulled away from their parents' house, Ella switched off the radio. "It's a short drive and I need to know a couple of things before we get there."

Faye just bet she did. "Only a couple?"

"I have a bunch of questions, obviously, but we only have time for two. First, were you frowning a while ago because you realized the costume stuff would mean less time with Gil?"

"Yes, but—"

"Then let's ditch using costumes. We'll tell Mrs. Allred we—"

"We're not ditching the costumes. You're right. I did think about Gil. But now I'm totally on board with costumes. They'll take the number from cute to amazing. You know how much I love putting on a crowd-pleasing production."

"I do know. Okay, the costumes are a go. Second question, *how was it*?"

Faye laughed. "How was what?"

"Stop it. You know what I'm asking. I didn't want to bring it up in front of the rest, but—"

"Thank you for that. I wouldn't have said much if you had brought it up."

"But now it's just you and me, so spill, sis."

"He's the most incredible lover I've ever had."

Ella whooped. "I knew it! Sandy and Danny. You guys were giving off sparks ten years ago. I just wish — well, never mind about that. What happened between you two, anyway?"

"That's three questions."

"I know, but we still have to park and get out. Plus we're here a little early." She pulled into the mostly empty parking lot, shut off the motor and turned to her. "Whatever he did must have been egregious for you to carry a grudge that long."

"It wasn't a grudge. It was... I've always been attracted to him, and after what happened, I wasn't going to risk... but in the end—"

"Did you have sex? Was that it?"

"Once. It was my first time. And his, too, but I didn't know that until Saturday night."

"*This* Saturday night? Two days ago?"

"Yes, when we had a long talk in his kitchen. When I found out he was a virgin, too, and humiliated by his terrible performance, which was why he didn't get in touch after that night… it took away the icky feelings about that night."

Ella's eyes flashed and her mouth flattened into a thin line. "He should have contacted you."

"He admits that. He feels terrible about it, even now."

"Good. Please tell me he's groveling."

"I guess you could say that."

"A lot? Because he needs to grovel a lot. And if he's not doing that, I have a few things I'd like to say to—"

"Ella. Do not call him out."

"He put you through hell! For years! Whose idea was it to keep the whole thing secret? His, I'll bet. I really want to let him know what I—"

"Don't you dare. Keeping it secret was a joint decision. And like I said, he feels terrible. He didn't know it was my first time until he hit some resistance. Then it was too late."

"And he should have effing called you!"

"See? This is why it's good I didn't tell you back when it happened. No telling what kind of revenge you would have dreamed up."

"Revenge is still on the table, kiddo. The statute of limitations hasn't expired."

"Yes, it has. Besides, I can tell he's really crazy about me, and he's liable to have a tough time when this week ends. In case that makes you feel any better."

"It kinda does. He deserves to suffer. But you don't. Will you have a tough time?"

"Maybe a little. I might stock up on Oreos so I'll have them if I need them. But right after I get back the semester will start and I'll be doing what I love. I'll be totally involved with those wonderful kids. We'll be creating so much magic on a daily basis that I'll forget all about Gil McLintock." At least that was her plan.

"And you'll have some hot memories for cold winter nights?"

"Smokin' memories." Her cheeks grew warm. "He was a big disappointment ten years ago, but now he's got it going on. I wouldn't miss this chance for anything."

"In that case, I'll butt out."

"Please do. I've got this."

<u>**25**</u>

Ten minutes past four according to the clock hanging on the shop wall. Fifty to go before Gil could ring the doorbell of the house where Faye had grown up.

All those years she'd lived in Wagon Train, been in his grade from kindergarten on. How could he have been so oblivious?

"It's a mystery, kitty-cat."

Rivet lay sprawled on the computer desk, eyes half-closed, probably bored because neither of her humans had lit up a torch today. That crazy calico loved the smell of hot metal, but she was out of luck this week. He and Bret had put a hold on projects until after the wedding.

Gil had expected the week of Marsh's wedding to be busy. He hadn't counted on needing a spreadsheet to keep track of his schedule. But since he was minding the shop for another thirty minutes or so and nobody was around besides Rivet, he'd turned on the computer to create one so he wouldn't lose track of his obligations.

Spending private time with Faye could easily blot out everything else if he didn't have his week mapped out. Forgetting the trip to Missoula was a prime example.

First up was scheduling Faye time. She'd laugh if he told her she was at the top of his To-Do list. Was he at the top of hers? He'd rather not speculate.

They'd had a couple of text exchanges this afternoon. She'd told him about the costumes she and Ella had picked up from the drama department's storage unit. She'd mentioned that some might need repairing. He had a memory of her sitting with a needle and thread, laboring over a poodle skirt.

Fortunately, she'd green-lighted the plan he'd worked out with Bret, who'd agreed to spend mornings in the shop and let him take afternoons. Faye would either ride in with him at noon if she had stuff to do in town or hang out with Ella at the ranch.

But in the morning, they could take their time. Heat settled in his groin as he contemplated what that meant. Well, unless she had to work on poodle skirts.

Not that he was totally free, either. Since he'd be in the shop every afternoon, he'd had to reschedule tomorrow's shoeing appointment from two in the afternoon to eleven in the morning. He had another one at ten on Wednesday.

That still left time for fooling around before he had to head out. Faye had indicated she'd like to tag along on his appointments. He'd enjoy that. On Thursday, barring the unexpected, they'd have the entire morning together.

He wanted it that way, because after that things would get tight. He added the dress rehearsal for *Summer Nights* on Thursday and the rehearsal dinner on Friday. Would she stay with him Friday morning? No telling, so he left Friday morning blank.

Friday night she'd likely go back to her folks' house. Of course he'd see her at the wedding and reception, but then…. yeah. Sunday.

He saved the file and shut down the computer. "Rivet, it's highly likely I've shot myself in the foot." He checked on the cat, who stared at him as if she completely agreed with that assessment. "Or maybe I shot myself higher up. I'm not gonna find anybody else who affects me like that woman."

He wasn't specific as to whether *higher up* meant his groin or his heart. Both were in the line of fire.

Rivet stretched a paw in his direction. "Thanks for the support, kitty." He took her paw and gently massaged the spaces between the leathery pads until her claws peeked out.

Her soft purr soothed the uneasiness in his gut. He'd made the right choice getting into this arrangement. No question about that. And he'd done his best to simulate the potential fallout. No sugar-coating allowed.

He sighed and slowly released Rivet's paw. "Just gotta live it, kitty-cat. Live it and see what happens." He stood and walked to the back room to fix Rivet's dinner before he left.

That inspired her to leap off the table and wind around his ankles while he dished it out. He set her bowl on the mat, refreshed her water dish and grabbed his keys. "Have a good night, kitty."

Plucking his hat from the rack next to the door, he put it on as he walked out. Then he paused before closing the door and called out to Rivet. "By the way, if you want to put it on your calendar, you'll be at my place this weekend. I need the company more than Bret does."

He locked the door and headed for the truck. Did Faye like cats? Not that it mattered. Chances were good she'd never meet Rivet. He made the short drive to her house in record time and parked in front since her sedan was sitting in the driveway.

The clock on his dash informed him he was four minutes early. He put the windows down. Might as well sit here until—

The front door opened and Faye stuck her head out. "Come on in! Dad wants to talk to you."

Oh, dear God. "Sure! Be right there!" His stomach pitched. Then he took a deep breath. He was twenty-eight, not eighteen. That put him way past the age where his girlfriend's father could call him on the carpet. Didn't it?

But this was Doc Bradley, one of the most respected people in town. He'd delivered a fair share of the town's babies, including him. Which made him responsible for the foreskin issue! Maybe the guy wanted to apologize.

More likely he wanted to remind Gil that he'd better use that part of his anatomy responsibly or there'd be hell to pay. Gil liked Doc Bradley. He'd just rather not have a conversation with the good doc right now.

Faye gave him a bright smile as she ushered him in the house. She was wearing flip-flops and her toes were painted a combination of teal and white. A small suitcase sat by her feet, so at least the program hadn't been scrapped. He just had to pay his dues.

She gestured toward the hallway. "He's in his study. First door on your right."

Nodding, he took off his hat.

"Let me take that."

"Thanks. I'll keep it." Lectures were best survived if you had something to hold onto.

"Don't worry." She lowered her voice. "He wants to talk to you about a gate."

"Fat chance."

"No, really."

"Sure." He flashed her what he hoped was a jaunty smile, squared his shoulders and marched down the hall, a full confession rolling through his head. *Yes, sir, I plan to have sex all week with your daughter and no, I won't be asking her to marry me. And by the way, I'm also the guy who broke her heart ten years ago. Would you like to clean my clock now or later?*

"Hey, Gil." Doc Bradley got up from behind an old, battered desk and came forward, hand outstretched. "Good to see you."

"Good to see you, sir." The handshake wasn't a bone-crusher. Good sign.

Ending the handshake, the good doctor moved past him and quietly closed the door.

Bad sign. And what was that rattling sound? He glanced over his shoulder. A full-sized skeleton hung from a hook on the back of the door. Probably one of Faye's old boyfriends.

He faced her dad and cleared his throat. "Before you say anything, sir, let me assure you I have tremendous respect for your daughter. She's a really amazing person and I would never—"

"Whoa, son." He held up both hands. "Did you think I called you in here for *the talk*?" He made air quotes.

"Yes, sir."

"Well, I hate to disappoint you, but Liz filled me in on the situation and clearly you and Faye are in complete agreement on how you want to handle your relationship. I suppose I could warn you not to break her heart if that's what you want to hear, but I know my daughter. I'd say you're equally at risk."

He gulped. "Yes, sir. So why did you—"

"I'm hoping to surprise Liz for our anniversary in October and I know she'd love a front gate. Something like the Carter's, but different. We can talk about the design later, but I'd like to get on your schedule. I've heard you and Bret are crazy busy."

"Yes, sir." That seemed to be his catch phrase for this episode.

"With that in mind, can you make me a gate between now and October eleventh?"

"Yes, sir. I mean, absolutely. Completely doable."

"Great! I'll be in touch after the wedding. And remember, it's a surprise. The girls know, but don't say anything in front of Liz."

"I won't, sir."

"All things considered, I think you should call me Gerald."

"All things considered, I'd like to stick with Doc Bradley. Sir."

He chuckled. "Okay." Then the laughter faded and the famous Doc Bradley compassion shone in his gaze. "Believe it or not, I understand why you and Faye have made this choice." He paused. "But it's too bad you can't... well, anyway, if you can at least be friends, that'll be a win."

"Yes, sir. And I'd better head out before that response becomes a permanent tic."

Grinning, Faye's dad shook his hand again. "See you at the rehearsal dinner."

"Yes—" He caught himself. "Yes, you will." He opened the door carefully, but the skeleton still knocked against it. "Is this real or plastic?"

"Real. His name's Danny Zuco."

"Whose idea was that?"

"Faye's."

"I see." He walked back to the front door where she stood waiting. "You were right about why he wanted to see me."

"So no lecture about doing right by his precious daughter?"

"No, ma'am." He put on his hat and picked up her suitcase. "Instead I got to meet Danny Zuco."

"Oh! I always forget about him." She opened the door and started out.

"I understand you're the one who came up with the name."

"Just for the fun of it. I mean, when your father brings home a skeleton you have to name him, right?"

He followed her down the walkway. "You could have named him Clyde."

"He doesn't look like a Clyde."

"But he looks like a Danny Zuco?" He set down the suitcase, opened the passenger door and helped her in, taking note that her fingernails matched her toes. Nudging back his hat, he braced his arm on the roof of the truck and gazed at her. "Did you hate me that much?"

"For a while."

His breath hitched. "I really did a number on you. Bret's still outraged on your behalf, by the way."

"You told him?"

"This morning on the way to Missoula. He's surprised you're willing to have sex with me. After meeting Danny Zuco, so am I." He made himself say it. "Are you sure this is a good idea?"

26

Faye had a glib answer on the tip of her tongue, something along the lines of *Hell, yeah! Damn the torpedoes! Full steam ahead!* But the depth of concern in Gil's blue eyes made her hesitate. "I can't answer for you, but for me it's a very good idea."

"I desperately want to believe that. If Oreos and *Bonanza* will get you through, then fine. But ten years ago I told myself you'd be fine. My justification for not calling was that it would only upset you more. Leaving you alone seemed like the right thing to do."

"It wasn't then, but it will be this time."

"You don't want me to keep in touch?"

"Not really. At least not at first, when we're readjusting to our normal lives. We can catch up at the reunion."

"The reunion? Two months?"

She gazed at him. "We just spent ten years not talking." Sitting in his truck breathing in the healthy male scent of him as he leaned close, she didn't know how she'd stayed away.

"I know, but that was before we… okay, you're right. We'll need some time to adjust back to a strictly friendship mode."

"I plan to throw myself into my work."

"Me, too, which I can, but your classes don't start yet, right?"

"Not quite, but like I said before, a few eager beavers and I will get a jump on the semester's projects. We tend to work late into the night so it'll be an excellent diversion."

"Then you might not need those Oreos and *Bonanza* after all."

"Probably not. That's an old coping mechanism I dug out to impress you when you told me you might drink 'til you puke. I felt I needed to describe something similar."

He smiled. "That's not similar."

"It is if I toss my cookies."

"Ha, ha. I doubt you eat Oreos and barf them up again."

"Depends on whether the *Bonanza* episode has a plot hole you could drive a truck through." She reached up and stroked his chin, slightly scratchy from late afternoon stubble. "The point is what it's always been. I'm not that vulnerable teenaged girl who was at loose ends after graduation."

"Intellectually I know this isn't anything like last time, but—"

"And you're not that teenaged boy, either." She could still see the eighteen-year-old in his eyes and his grin, but she preferred this slightly battle-scarred version. "I never asked how your summer went that year."

"Not good. Lots of self-blame. Ducking around corners whenever I saw you in town."

She moved her hand down and toyed with a button on his shirt. He'd left the top two undone. Judging from his tan, it was a habit. "I got so I could recognize you from fifty yards away and make a run for it."

"Not if I saw you first."

"What an exhausting three months. I swore I'd never spend another summer in Wagon Train."

His eyes widened. "*That's* why you got into the Shakespeare summer program up in Washington?"

"Yes, and before you apologize, don't. It's been fabulous, and I might not have done it if I hadn't been desperate to get away from you. I'm grateful."

"You're welcome, I guess." He sighed. "In other words, avoiding me has had benefits."

"Huge benefits. When I needed a legitimate excuse to skip the five-year-reunion, I volunteered to help organize a community theater production of *The Legend of Sleepy Hollow.* Now they do it every year and it's so much fun."

"Then it's not just your classes that keep you busy? You volunteer, too?"

"Why not when I love it so much?"

"Yeah, but you said you'd be at this year's reunion. Will the *Sleepy Hollow* gig keep you from—"

"No. They can manage without me this once. Don't worry, I'll be at the reunion."

"Will you be okay by then? It won't bother you?"

"I should be fine. How about you?"

"I'll be okay if you are. It's good to know you'll have so much going on."

"I'm not saying I won't miss you, or that my heart won't ache. Or other parts won't ache when I remember how good it was."

The light in his eyes changed and his throat moved in a slow swallow. "Yeah, me, too."

"But I think we decided the rewards are worth the price."

"We did. And speaking of those rewards... shall we take off?"

Her body heated. "Wonderful idea."

Pushing away from the truck, he picked up her suitcase and stashed it behind her seat, while she pulled the door closed and buckled up.

Moments later he climbed in, fastened his seatbelt and turned the key. "Can I assume you won't be naming any skeletons after me this time around?"

"I didn't name that one after you."

He pulled away from the curb. "Only because your family would have freaked out if you'd tried to name him Gil McLintock."

"Oh, my God, I wouldn't have done that! Not in a million years. That's so creepy."

"And naming him Danny Zuco isn't?"

"Maybe a little, but Danny's fictional. I'm pretty sure I thought of it as getting revenge on the character. It made some kind of crazy sense to blame him for the mess we got into."

"He probably had something to do with it. Sandy did, too."

"Are you saying you fell for Sandy?"

"Hook, line and sinker."

"Then I should probably warn you I have both her wigs. Or rather, Ella has them in her truck, along with a whole bunch of costumes."

"You planning on wearing the curly one at some point?"

"What do you think? Of course."

"Which means you're doing more than one number on Friday night."

"That's my new goal. I'd have to do a fast costume change from the poodle skirt to the black outfit, but I can manage that."

"Will you fit into it now that you're—"

"Oh, yeah. The top was a little loose back then. I had to pin it. I'll fill it out way better now."

He gave her an arched-brow glance. "I'm in for it, aren't I?"

"Yep. Are you man enough to sing *You're the One That I Want* with me?"

"Looks like I'd better be. If I don't give myself something to do, I'll be the guy in the audience with a napkin draped across his lap and another one handy to wipe the drool off his chin."

She glanced away to hide a smile. Costumes had been *such* a good idea. Silly her for balking. "That number's more demanding than *Summer Nights*."

"I'm aware of that."

"We should probably practice on our own before Thursday night."

"In costume?"

"Would you like that?" She knew the answer but she wanted to hear him say it.

"I believe I would."

She shivered in anticipation of what this night might bring. "I found the black sleeveless T-shirt you wore for that one. And the tight black pants."

"Oh, you did, did you?"

"If I'm wearing my costume, you need to wear yours."

"I dunno. I might split the seams of that shirt."

"You won't. It's stretchy. You'll just fill it out more." She gave him a smile. "Can't wait to see it on you."

"And where are these costumes, again? I know you told me, but this conversation is frying my brain cells."

"In Ella's truck. Want me to ask her to bring them over?"

"Sounds good. I'm liking this private practice idea."

"I can tell. But remember, we can't rip off these valuable costumes like we might if they were our clothes."

He gave her a panty-melting glance. "I'm capable of a slow peel."

"I'm texting her." One previously improbable fantasy, coming up.

<u>27</u>

Gil surveyed the garment bags layered on his sofa and the hat and shoe boxes stacked on the floor. He hadn't been able to resist the idea of a private practice, in costume, no less. Looked like tonight Faye would discover just how much he'd kept up his skills.

Ella had come and gone quickly, saying Marsh was making dinner. "Your sister seemed a little frosty towards me. Did you tell her about—"

"I did. You're not her favorite person right now, but she'll come around. It's a good thing I didn't tell her when it happened. Your summer would have taken a decided turn for the worse."

"She's entitled. She's your big sister and I treated you like crap."

"But not anymore, and she liked you before. She's marrying your brother. It'll be fine."

"She can be mad at me for as long as she wants." He gestured toward the pile of garment bags. "Did you guys clean out the place?"

"Not by a long shot." Faye sorted through the bags, consulted a tag and pulled one out. "The drama department rents a good-sized storage unit. We won't need all these, but I wanted to increase the odds I could outfit anyone who chooses to wear a costume."

"You said some of them will need repairing."

"They will, and doing it will help Mrs. Allred. I'll also make a donation."

"So will I. This is generous of her. Shows how much she trusts you."

"And I will be *very* careful." She unzipped the bag she'd located and unhooked something black from its hanger.

"Is that your top?"

"Nope. Yours." She handed him the sleeveless T-shirt.

He took it by the shoulders and held it up. "Wow. Sure brings back memories."

"Sure does."

He liked the way she was looking at him, but Ella's comment about Marsh making dinner reminded him that he needed to get with that program. He'd invited Faye to stay with him which meant feeding her in addition to the other activities they had planned.

He draped the shirt over the back of an easy chair. "All this can wait. We need to eat."

"I'll go along with that." She pulled black pants out of the bag. "But first put these with your shirt."

He laid the folded pants on top of the T-shirt. "Good thing I kept those black loafers."

"You still have them?" She looked as if he'd announced she'd won the lottery. "That's fabulous! I brought whatever black loafers I could find, but I doubt any would fit you right, especially since you have to dance in them. I'm guessing you still have a sentimental attachment to those shoes."

"I do." And he used them so much in the past ten years he'd had to have them resoled. He could tell her that now and blow her away, but it would be more fun to have her discover the truth when they started dancing.

Those shoes were like the ring, a connection to her, to a special time and a special relationship that he'd cherished and then ruined. "In any case, I'll haul them out later. Right now, I'm headed for the kitchen. You're welcome to come with me or keep sorting."

"I'll come with you. Put me to work."

He took her at her word and they shared the chopping duties while they put together a stir-fry. The routine was strangely familiar.

She let out a sigh. "I like being in your kitchen."

"I like having you here." He added the final ingredients and turned the stirring over to her while he made the sauce. "You and your fancy fingers and toes."

"Like 'em?" She wiggled her hand and held out her foot.

"Very much. Can you dance in flop-flops?"

"Not well. I brought some shoes that should work and not mess up the pedicure."

"I'll be careful not to step on your toes."

"You always were. Think you can still do the moves?"

"I think so. By the way, how many hours of costume repair do you think you have?"

"I won't know until I get into it. That's something I can do here while you're at the shop, though. I won't let it cut into our time together."

"I'd offer to help but other than sewing on a button, I wouldn't be much use."

"Besides, we have better things to do with our private time."

"Like practice our song and dance routine?"

"Like that." She gave him a sideways glance. "And whatever happens afterward."

His cock twitched. "If you're trying to get me hot, it's working."

"Glad to hear it."

"But we're eating first."

"Damn straight. This smells delicious."

"So do you, but I'm leaving it at that. No more sexy talk." He handed her the sauce. "Drizzle this over it and turn down the heat."

"On me or the stir-fry?"

"Both, sassy-pants. What if you don't have enough time for the repairs?"

"I think I will."

"You could ask the Wenches. Teresa quilts and Colleen knits and crochets."

"Right! I knew that. Teresa made Ella and Marsh a gorgeous quilt and Colleen gave them a super-soft afghan. I'll ask them. Thanks for the idea."

"Anytime. We're done. I'll get the plates."

"Can we just eat in here?"

"You bet." He set the plates on the counter. "I have wine if you—"

"Yes, please."

"Red or white?"

"Red."

"Good choice. Want to dish us up while I open it?"

"Will do."

In no time they'd taken their seats across from each other. He raised his glass. "To our first meal together."

"Is it? That can't be right. For one thing, we all went for pizza after the final performance."

"That doesn't count. We ended up at opposite ends of a very long table."

"We spent most of Senior Ditch Day together. I'm sure there was food involved."

"Do you remember sitting near each other while we ate? Because I sure don't."

"Me, either. I remember lots of silly games, goofing around, water balloons...."

"Oh, God. The water balloons. But you see my point. This is our first actual shared meal."

"Guess so." She touched her glass to his. "To our first meal together, one we even cooked together."

"Yes, we did." He held her gaze as he sipped. Then he put down his glass and picked up his fork. "I've been wondering something."

She finished chewing and swallowed. "Me, too. When are you going to open a restaurant? This is amazing."

"I'll open one if you'll run it with me. I've never cooked that effortlessly with anyone."

She flushed. "Really?"

"Have you?"

"No, but then I don't generally cook with someone else."

"Which brings me to my question. With your demanding job and your volunteering, when do you have time to date?"

Her flush deepened. "I really don't. That was one of the issues with the guy who moved to New York. He said I never had time for him. He thought if we went to New York, it would shake up the dynamic. I knew it wouldn't."

"Then you made the right call." He dug into his meal, which was darned good, maybe the best version of this dish he'd made so far.

"He said my work was more important to me than he was."

Still chewing, he looked up.

She'd stopped eating. Evidently he'd touched a nerve. He finished chewing and swallowed. Waited to see if she'd say more.

"He was right, Gil. My work has been more important than any of the guys I've dated, which is why those relationships all fizzled."

He put down his fork. This was important. "Do you think that will always be the case?"

"I... maybe... I do love it. Look at this week, for example. I'm here for my sister's wedding and yet this afternoon I raided the high school drama department's storage unit for costumes. I've talked you into doing a second number with me."

"You didn't have to do much talking. I'm excited about it, and not just because we're going to practice tonight and then have mind-blowing sex."

She smiled. "If you had any idea how many times I've dreamed about—"

"You're not alone. It's been my fantasy for years."

"And the Universe cooperated to give us this opportunity to make it come true."

"I think it was my mother, but then again, she's a force of nature. I've always figured she was in league with the Universe."

"I'd agree with you." She loaded her fork with another bite of the stir-fry. "Eat up. You're going to need the fuel for what lies ahead."

"Yes, ma'am." He was happy to go with the flow, leave the subject alone for now. But her answer to his big question hadn't really been an answer. Would she always choose her work over a relationship with a guy?

He didn't think so. And he had the evidence to prove it. *I won't let it cut into our time together.* She cared about this Friday night production. But it wasn't more important than the time they'd carved out for themselves. She was guarding that for all she was worth.

But mentioning it might backfire. He'd much rather have her discover it on her own, but that could take time. And time was in short supply.

<u>28</u>

Faye insisted on changing into their costumes separately. For maximum impact, she'd make an entrance the way Sandy had in the musical. They'd pushed back the furniture in the living room, including the sofa heavy with garment bags, to give them a dance floor. He would dress in there and she'd use his room.

Turned out he happened to have the soundtrack on his phone and he had a couple of wireless speakers. They'd simply sing over Olivia Newton-John and John Travolta. It wasn't elegant but it would get the job done. Would they remember the choreography Mrs. Allred had created? If not, they'd improvise.

She walked into his bedroom carrying her outfit and a hatbox containing the curly wig. Laying them on the bed, she switched on both bedside lamps. The time for dark trysts was over.

He'd made the bed at some point during his busy day, but it was a hasty job. Just looking at the slightly rumpled quilt sent ripples of awareness through her lady parts. She stripped off everything but her panties and tucked her clothes in an outside pocket of her suitcase.

The black top had a built-in bra. Ten years ago she'd stuffed tissues into it to give her cleavage. No tissues required this time.

Once she'd poured herself into the slinky outfit with no room to spare, she dug her red heels out of her suitcase and sat on a straight-backed chair in the corner to strap them on. Last, but certainly not least, she grabbed the hat box and headed into the bathroom.

She'd checked the wig this afternoon and clearly nobody had used it since she'd put it away after the final performance ten years ago. The wig cap was tucked in with it along with the bobby pins that she'd left for the next wearer. Who would have guessed it would be her?

Mrs. Allred said the wig and outfit had gone unworn because no one felt worthy of it after Faye's spectacular job with this number. She'd become a legend.

Flattering as that was, the department was wasting perfectly good items. Maybe she'd drive down this fall and talk to the drama class. This stuff should be back in circulation.

In the meantime, it was hers for a week. She tied her hair in a low ponytail, lifted it over her head and secured it before pulling on the wig cap and the wig.

Taking a deep breath, she faced the mirror... and stared at her eighteen-year-old self. As if the emotions had clung to the costume, they came rushing back — fear, exhilaration, pride.

She'd reached the pinnacle, starring in her high school's biggest production of the year. And she'd been deeply, painfully, naively in love with her leading man. And he with her.

They'd botched their storybook ending that summer and that was for the best. She and Gil weren't destined for a happily-ever-after. But they sure as hell deserved a happy-for-now.

She fetched her cosmetic bag from her suitcase and refreshed her makeup. Tossing the bag back into the suitcase, she walked to the door and opened it, heart pounding. "Places!"

The first jazzy piano notes made her shiver in recognition. Throwing her head back, she sashayed out, ready to knock her co-star for a loop. But one look at Gil in his sleeveless black T-shirt and she forgot to breathe.

He froze, too, his eyes wide. John Travolta eyes. His chest heaved. And he began to sing, the sound clear and true. Danny's voice. He slipped into the role as if he'd performed it yesterday, executing the suggestive hip moves with ease.

That sandbagger! She'd bet her retirement fund he sang every day. And danced, too, judging from his limber demonstration. He didn't just *happen* to have the soundtrack on his phone.

She'd have to bring her A-game to keep up with him. No problem. She belted out her lyrics with the ballsy delivery she'd perfected ten years ago. Gil's blue eyes glittered and he smiled. Damn, he was sexy!

They took turns stalking each other, ramping up the energy, mirroring each other's steps. The invisible cord that had connected them on stage was back, gradually tightening until they were in each other's face, tempting, taunting, wild with hormone-driven needs.

He teased her with those swiveling hips and she gave it right back with a shimmy and a toss of her head. How she'd missed this! No one lit her up on stage like this guy.

When he started laughing, so did she. Joy bubbled up, joy and arousal in a heady combo that she hadn't known how to handle ten years ago. Oh, she could handle it now. She was a match for this cowboy. She couldn't wait to get her hands on him.

As the ending approached, he grabbed her around the waist and hoisted her up. She wound her legs around his hips and her arms around his neck. He kept dancing, twirling her around, his gaze locked with hers, that cocky grin on his handsome face.

The song was almost over. Breathing hard, he danced her over to his phone propped in its holder. "Get the phone." He dipped her toward it.

She snatched it up as the opening bars of *Sandy* filled the room. She gulped for air. "Want to… sing that?"

"Nope." He gasped. "Got something else in mind."

"Alrighty." She tapped the phone and cut off John Travolta's sad lament. "Sing that one much?"

"Who wants to know?" Still puffing, he carried her down the hall.

"The person who just saw you dance and sing like a pro. 'Fess up, McLintock."

"Not now."

"Later?"

"Much later." Moving into the bedroom, he put her down on the edge of the mattress and dropped to his knees. He glanced up, his hot gaze holding hers as he unbuckled her shoe without having to look.

Her breath hitched. It was a small thing, understanding the intricacies of a woman's footwear, but it said so much about the experiences he'd had in the years they'd been apart.

He eased her foot out of the shoe and set it aside. "I'm not—" He paused to clear the huskiness from his throat. "I'm not taking off your outfit."

"Why?"

"Don't trust myself. You'll have to."

"What about yours? Want me to—"

"I can handle mine." He set the other shoe aside and stood. "I didn't expect..." He sucked in a breath and shoved his hands through his damp hair. A Danny move. "I could rip it." He backed away.

The hunger in his eyes made a believer out of her. "I'll do it." Trembling, she got to her feet and pulled the hem of her top free.

He stood perfectly still, watching.

"Maybe you should start on yours."

"I will." He didn't move, didn't shift his attention.

Crossing her arms, she grasped the hem and tugged the top slowly over her head, freeing her breasts along the way. His audible swallow told her he was still watching. Leaning over, she turned the top inside out as she stripped it off her arms and looked up.

"You're so beautiful." His voice rasped in the silence.

She soaked in his words, the flush on his cheeks, the hunger in his eyes. "Thank you." She handed him the top. "Just put it over the back of the chair."

He turned, laying it carefully so it wouldn't slide off. Then he reached for the back of his shirt. His biceps flexed as he pulled it gently forward over his head and laid it on top of hers.

Such a powerful chest. The rhythm of their dance still coursed through her. She'd expected some missteps. Instead he'd thoroughly seduced her with a muscular, virile body that moved with the agility of youth. And made love with the finesse of experience.

He nudged off his loafers, shoes he'd clearly continued to dance in. Sitting in the chair, he pulled off his socks. White Danny Zuco socks.

When he got to his feet and reached for the button at the waistband of the tight-fitting pants, saliva pooled in her mouth.

He paused and looked at her, his blue eyes sparkling. "Gonna just stand there?"

Evidently she was capable of ogling, too. "No." She unbuttoned her pants but kept an eye on him because... why not?

"Zipper's got problems." He took his time dragging it down. "Don't want to break it."

"Looks like you're doing a striptease." She wiggled out of her pants, laid them on top of her suitcase and hopped into bed, shoving the covers to the foot of it. Now she could concentrate on him as he unveiled his manly attributes.

Or not. "It's stuck."

"You or the zipper?"

"The zipper. I'm not pulling it all the way down and risk breaking it. I can still get out of 'em, but it'll be tricky, for obvious reasons."

"Just don't injure anything important." The dance and the costumes had worked her into a lather and now she was foiled by the very costume that had excited her so much. By the time he'd extricated himself from those pants, she was hyperventilating.

Scooting over toward the bedside table, she took out a condom, so she'd have it ready when he finally abandoned those pants.

"That zipper's not right." He continued to focus on it as he stood there in all his naked, aroused glory. "You might want to check it out, see if you can make it slide easier."

"Now?"

"Oh, hell, no." Still fiddling with the zipper, he turned around, giving her a stunning view of his tight buns as he draped the pants over their shirts and tossed his briefs onto the chair seat. "I mean when you ladies are repairing—" He turned around and blinked. "You're in bed. When did you get in bed?"

"Hours ago."

"Are you okay? Your face is really pink."

"Because I'm dealing with a terminal case of lust and if you don't get over here immediately, I'll expire on the spot."

"Can't have that." He approached, clearly no longer distracted, his gaze traveling the length of her body. "Sorry to keep you waiting."

"Catch." She tossed him the condom.

He missed. Grinning, he paused and picked it up. "Sun was in my eyes."

"Tell the truth. It was the light bouncing off my curly hair." She fluffed it and gave him a come-hither smile.

"It was the light bouncing off all of you. I couldn't catch a multi-colored beach ball with you lying there all glowy."

"Too much?"

"Never." He rolled on the condom. "I don't want to do it in the dark ever again. I don't know what I was thinking last night."

"You were thinking do-over."

"Guess so. But now that the do-over's done, let's keep the lights on."

"Fine with me. Are you getting in or what?"

"Getting in." He settled beside her and pulled her close. "Dancing with you was amazing. Especially in that costume. The way you move... I wonder if you know what that does to me."

She trembled. "I didn't when we were younger. I do, now."

"I'm not sure you do. But I'm going to show you." Rolling her to her back, he captured her lips in an open-mouthed kiss, wedged his hips between her thighs and thrust deep.

<u>**29**</u>

Gil believed there had to be a way he and Faye could be together. He didn't know how, but he knew why... especially when he was buried up to the hilt, locked in an embrace that shot past anything he'd ever experienced.

The strength of his connection with Faye stunned him. And never more than tonight. Lifting slowly away from the kiss, he looked into her luminous eyes, warm like a summer rain.

He rocked his hips, pulling back a little and settling in again, nudging closer. "Every time I do that, it feels brand new."

Her breath hitched.

"But familiar. Like I'm where I'm supposed to be."

She slid her hands down his back and gripped his glutes. "You are."

"Because you asked me. You asked me with every swivel of your hips." He drew back and pushed forward, watching her eyes widen and her lips part as her breath quickened.

"Yes." Her whispered answer was almost a sigh.

"I accept your invitation, Faye." He began to stroke. "You came through loud and clear. You want me. You want this."

"*Yes.*" She dug her fingers into his flexing glutes.

"I could see it in the way you moved, the light in your beautiful eyes. And here I am, whenever you want me." He pumped faster. "All you have to do…" He gulped for air. "Is ask. Ask me, Faye. What do you want?"

"More…" Her moan was soft, yet urgent. "*More.*"

He bore down and she arched upward with a cry, her orgasm rolling over his cock, his heartbeat thrumming in his ears as he fought off the urge to let go.

"Come with me!"

Her gasping plea tore through the furious rhythm he'd created and shattered his control. With a groan of surrender he plunged into her pulsing channel and let the cyclone take him. It roared through his body, shaking him like a ragdoll.

No telling how long he stayed braced above her, eyes squeezed shut, struggling for breath.

Her soft hand caressing his cheek coaxed him to open his eyes. He looked down on the woman who'd stolen his heart.

She was smiling, her gaze tender. "I was afraid you'd go all macho on me and hold back so you could make me come again."

"That was the plan." He sounded like his vocal cords had rusted. "But then you asked and I couldn't very well refuse."

Her smile widened. "All I have to do is ask and you'll strip down and make me happy? And come on command?"

"Yes, ma'am."

"You may regret telling me that."

"It's always been true. I'm just making it official."

"That adds a whole new dimension to this week."

This week. His chest tightened. Should he tell her she'd misunderstood, that there was no expiration date on that promise? Better not.

Leaning down, he brushed his lips over hers. "Gotta make the condom run. See you soon."

"I'll be here, dreaming up ways to exercise my newly discovered power."

"Have fun." He kept his tone light. As he headed for the bathroom, he argued with himself. Didn't she see how good they were together? It hit him in the face every five seconds.

Did she think this kind of bonding was commonplace? Because it damn well wasn't. She should know that since none of her relationships had panned out.

Then it dawned on him. She wasn't working this week. It was a window of opportunity to fool around, but it wasn't how she lived in her normal day-to-day existence.

Could she make room for him in her life if they were somehow magically occupying the same geographical space? Or more to the point, would she? Maybe geography wasn't the main problem.

When he came back out, she'd propped pillows against the headboard, one set for her and another for him. "Are we having pillow talk time?"

"We are. Believe it or not, we've come to the *later* segment that you spoke of, the one where you explain to me why you nailed *You're the One That I Want.*"

"I suppose we have. Since we barely made a dent in that wine, what if I fetch that and some chocolate chip cookies?"

"You eat cookies in bed?"

"You don't?"

"Yes, but I brush off the crumbs before I go to sleep, or... do other stuff."

"You'll be shocked to learn I brush off the crumbs, too. Be right back." How someone handled cookie crumbs in bed was a small matter, not enough to base a relationship on. But small matters kept building up.

Loading a tray with wine, glasses, a plate of cookies and a couple of napkins, he returned to find the bed empty and Faye in the bathroom brushing her hair, her actual hair. He set the tray on the bedside table. "Ditched the wig?"

"I hope you don't mind." She put the brush down and came out. "My head was getting hot."

"I like your real hair better."

"That's very nice of you to say, but I heard from a reliable source that you fell for Sandy, and I quote, *hook, line and sinker.*"

"Turns out she's not real. Call me crazy, but I'd rather make love to you."

"Then you didn't pretend I was Sandy while we did the deed?"

"No. You were Faye wearing a blonde wig. Did you pretend I was Danny?"

"No!"

"Because my hair's not black?"

"Because Danny was kind of scrawny. You've bulked up, which is lovely to look at and delicious when we're skin-to-skin."

"I wasn't scrawny."

"Well, you didn't look like this!" She swept her hand to encompass him from head to foot.

"I suppose not."

"You have more chest hair, too. I like that. It feels good."

"Keep talking like that and we'll be postponing our pillow talk."

"Nope, nope. Pillow talk first, sex later. I'll get in and then you can hand me the tray while you get in."

"Seems like someone is familiar with this routine."

"Not the way you're thinking. Ella was the first one to get a TV in her room and we'd make snacks, get in her bed and watch movies."

"*Bonanza* reruns?"

"Sometimes." She got settled and held out her hands for the tray. "*How I Met Your Mother* was one of our favorites, but we've both always loved cowboys."

And she expected to end up with a professor? He got into bed carefully, leaving space between them for the tray.

She set it down and poured them each a half-glass of wine. "That way you're not as likely to spill it."

"Thanks." He spread a napkin in his lap, picked up a cookie and glanced over at her. "You're in charge of this pillow talk. What do you want to know?"

"How long have you been practicing?"

"I didn't get serious about it until I moved into this cabin. When I still lived at Mom's and nobody was around, I'd play the *Grease* soundtrack and do a little bit. Once I had my own place, I was free to practice as much as I wanted."

"Why?"

"You're not eating your cookie."

"Because this is fascinating, Gil." She took a sip of her wine. "Okay, I'll eat my cookie while you explain why you continue to polish your skills when you never intend for anyone to know."

"It's my hobby. It's good exercise and it makes me happy. I've branched out by watching other musicals. I've taught myself some of those routines, too."

"But why the secrecy?"

"Bret, mostly. He could easily misinterpret it as frustration because I wish I'd become a star. I don't. Also, there's no venue here, so why tell anyone? Some guys work out. I'd rather do this."

She munched on another cookie, then she put it down. "So by setting up this rehearsal dinner gig, I'll be blowing your cover."

"Maybe, unless you'll help me convince everyone you were able to whip me into shape after a ten-year break."

"That'll be a tough sell. Besides, your mother's invited Mrs. Allred to the rehearsal dinner so she can see how the performance turns out."

"I should have seen that coming."

"Bottom line, if you perform on Friday night the way you just did in your living room, you'll cause a stir. Folks will ask questions. The truth will come out."

"I know. That's why I have to talk to Bret and hope to hell he believes me."

"I think he will. I do. I'm glad you're doing this for yourself. Then again, I'm also the only person who knows you considered making a career of it."

He sighed. "I might not tell Bret that."

"Your secret's safe with me."

"That I know. Ten years and you didn't crack."

"Guess I don't have to worry about your performance at the reunion. You'll knock 'em dead."

"*We'll* knock 'em dead."

"And, you'll have the reunion venue every five years."

"Only if you'll commit to doing it with me each time." He gazed at her.

She hesitated.

He wasn't about to let her off the hook. If she was beginning to realize their futures were linked and she'd be dealing with him for the rest of her life, fine with him.

"Okay, I'll agree to that." She drained her wine glass and set it on the tray. "And now that we've had our pillow talk and snacks, it's time to brush off the crumbs."

"Ready to go to sleep?"

"I'm ready to activate that anytime, anywhere provision you instituted a while ago."

Heat traveled immediately to his groin. "You're asking?"

"I'm asking."

<u>30</u>

Staying with Gil for a few days had been an exciting prospect even before she found out he'd kept his song and dance skills sharp. Now that he'd demonstrated his dedication to that activity, their interaction changed dramatically.

Although she sang all the time in her Missoula apartment, she'd been shy about doing it as Gil's houseguest. His request for *Hopelessly Devoted to You* had felt like a one-time thing, not an invitation to randomly burst into song.

His revelation changed all that. Singing was happening, sometimes together, sometimes solo, and on the drive to his shoeing appointment, they rocked out to country tunes.

Observing him while sitting on a camp stool in the shade, she learned a fair amount about his job, including the fact that he thoroughly enjoyed it. She also discovered he sang softly to calm the horses as he fit them with new shoes.

On the way back, he turned down the volume on the radio. "What did you think?"

She thought he looked scrumptious in a sweat-dampened T-shirt, but that wasn't what he was asking. "It was fun to watch. I've never seen the process except once in a video. I'm so glad you let me tag along."

"Anytime. Enjoyed the company."

"But I could tell you would have been fine without it. The job suits you. For what it's worth, I agree you made the right choice ten years ago."

"Can I call on you for backup if I have trouble convincing Bret?"

"Absolutely. When are you going to talk to him?"

"I haven't figured that out. Since we've split shop duty, we're not in there at the same time."

"Maybe you could ask him to stop by the shop during one of your afternoon stints. It probably needs to be before Thursday night."

"Whoa. Thursday night. I have it on my schedule and I still forgot until you just said it."

She smiled. "You've been busy."

"Yes, ma'am." He gave her a hot glance. "Tired of me, yet?"

"Not even slightly."

"Probably a good thing I have shop duty this afternoon, though." He grinned. "Gives you a chance to miss me."

"Which I promise I will."

"I'll miss you, too. But if Bret can stop by today, that'll be good."

"Bet you didn't expect any of this when you lured me to your cabin Saturday night."

"Lured you?"

"What else would you call it? You dangled a mysterious souvenir as bait."

"And you took that bait."

"Literally."

"And here we are." He reached over and squeezed her knee. "I don't regret a thing. Not for a second."

"Me, either. And by the way, thank you for letting me host the Wenches at your place this afternoon."

"I'd turn my cabin over to the Wenches anytime." He glanced at the clock on the dash. "We're running late. You'll need to welcome them while I grab a shower."

"Okay. Will you have time to eat some of the lunch they're bringing?"

"Only if it's something I can take with me."

"I'll let them know. I'm sure we can come up with a to-go meal while you're in the shower."

"How many will be there?"

"Everybody except Jess. She's working on a feature for the *Sentinel* and she also told me she never learned to sew. But she gave me her measurements so I can find her a poodle skirt. Angie and Molly are dropping by later to try some on."

"Then my mom's coming?"

"She is. Are you surprised?"

"Kinda. She's not much for needlework. She taught us how to sew on a button and I think that's the extent of her knowledge."

"That's a worthwhile skill. I noticed plenty of loose buttons."

"Don't forget to check out the zipper on my pants."

She giggled. "Are you sure you want me to take care of that this afternoon?"

He flushed. "Oh. I guess not. I just don't want to struggle with it Friday night."

"I'll make sure it won't be an issue." On the one hand, she couldn't wait to see how the performance turned out. On the other… their week together would be over.

* * *

When Faye asked the Wenches if they could create a to-go lunch for Gil, they put one together immediately. Minutes later he walked into the kitchen, his hair still damp from the shower, and they fussed over him like fond aunties. He soaked it up.

She got a kick out of seeing him surrounded by adoring women, probably because they were all Desiree's age. But someday he'd be smiling and laughing with a girlfriend. Quite likely his next serious relationship would lead to marriage.

For ten years she'd avoided being present for that potential scenario. Time was up. He'd find someone wonderful, and she wanted that for him.

He'd bring his new love to a family gathering and Faye was determined she'd be among the first to offer her congratulations. She wasn't ready to face such a moment now, but when it came, she would be.

Gil finally got out the door with his lunch and the Wenches took over his kitchen. The fairy godmother image still held. They'd shown up wearing T-shirts in their signature colors and lunch appeared like magic. Although no one had a magic wand, cleanup afterward was breathtakingly quick.

Then the party moved to the living room and everyone took a garment bag to ferret out the clothes that needed attention. Teresa set up an assembly line worthy of Henry Ford and Faye took a supervisory role.

The Wenches worked so efficiently that she had to ask. "Have you all done this before?"

Colleen, whose red shirt said *Sew What?*, glanced at her. "For the past nine years."

"You started the year after I graduated?"

"We did," Desiree said. "I didn't find out until after *Grease* was over that Carolyn could have used some extra help with the costumes. We were too late for that production, but we told her to call on us the next time."

"And it's fun." Cindy, sporting red, white and blue hair for the upcoming Labor Day, spread a poodle skirt over her lap. "So we kept doing it."

"Does Gil know? When he suggested I ask you it didn't sound like he had any idea."

"He probably doesn't," his mom said. "We don't make a big deal of it. We just like helping out."

"Although this school year could be the last time." Nancy glanced at Desiree with a look that was strangely like a signal. "We'll have to see how it goes after that."

"Is something changing?"

"Yes." Desiree met her gaze. "But it's not widely known. Carolyn's retiring at the end of the year."

Faye gasped. "She is? Well, I suppose I shouldn't be surprised. She's been there as long as

I can remember. I just can't imagine the drama department without her."

"We can't, either," Annette said. "The school's keeping it quiet for now. It's the juniors who'll feel it the most and there's no reason to say anything until... well, until they've found a replacement the kids can get excited about."

"I can't imagine who that would be. Talk about big shoes to fill. I..." She glanced around the room and felt a little sick to her stomach. "Is there a reason you're telling me this?"

"Yes." Desiree looked her in the eye. "And just so you know, ever since you contacted us about the costumes this morning, we've been hotly debating whether to tell you. The majority voted in favor."

She pressed a hand to her stomach. "Is this about Gil?"

"It can't very well *not* be about Gil," Desiree said. "Not now, anyway, but your name came up even before you and Gil made your announcement. The administration's talked with Carolyn to get recommendations and you were at the top of the list."

"But she didn't say a word yesterday."

"Because we warned her there was a complication and you might view this prospect as manipulation, which I promise it's not. In view of that, she told us to use our own judgment about telling you."

"And we decided you should know," Teresa said.

She swallowed. "You don't understand. In May I turned in my paperwork to apply for tenure.

I've worked hard to become eligible. My chances are good, especially since I've been very successful with grant proposals."

"Tenure's not easy to get," Nancy said. "My sister worked her tail off. Took years."

"Tenure's not the only thing, maybe not even the most important thing. I have a dream job. My colleagues are great and the students are awesome. I'm also the only one in the department who's good at writing grants, which we desperately need."

"You'd have a year to teach someone how to write grants," Desiree said gently. "It's not like this would take place tomorrow."

"Or ever." She took a deep breath and focused on Desiree. "I assume Gil doesn't know about this."

"Of course not. And he won't unless you choose to tell him. That's totally up to you."

"Thank you for that." She surveyed the room and saw only kindness and empathy. "I understand why you'd all like me to take the job. You love the school and you love Gil."

"But it has to be the right thing for you," Annette said. "You're the only one who knows what that is."

"I am." She took another deep breath. "And I don't see it happening."

31

Gil couldn't wait to get home to Faye. He forced himself to slow down on the ranch road because this time of day critters would be out.

He hadn't forgotten that he only had three nights left with her. But he refused to dwell on it. Not tonight. Every moment he spent with her increased his chances of finding a solution that would allow them to be together.

She might be leaving at the end of the week, but she wasn't gone yet. And he planned to make every minute count.

He turned down his road and was relieved to see an empty parking area. The Wenches had left and he'd have Faye all to himself until his appointment tomorrow morning. Judging from her reaction to the one this morning, she'd opt to go again. Evidently she hadn't been bored.

Parking, he quickly exited the truck. Should he have brought her something from town? Flowers, maybe? Or picked up something special to make for dinner? He had stuff, but he could have stopped at the market and picked up something extra plus a bouquet of flowers.

Too late, now. He'd consider it for tomorrow night. He could find a subtle way to find out if she even liked getting flowers. Come to think of it, they were sort of a cliché.

Bounding up the steps, he crossed the porch in two strides and opened the door. He almost called out *honey, I'm home* but thought better of it.

As she came toward him, he took one look at her face and was glad he hadn't used that corny greeting. "What's wrong?"

She swallowed. "I don't know where to start."

His gut churned. "That bad, huh? Is it about the performance?"

"No."

"The wedding?"

"No. It's..." She made a vague gesture toward the sofa, where garment bags were neatly stacked. "It's something I found out from the Wenches."

He debated whether to pull her into his arms. Didn't seem like she'd welcome that, though. "Let's go in the kitchen and grab a couple of bottles of cider."

"Okay." She walked ahead of him through the doorway, her steps listless.

What could the Wenches have told her? He'd left a smiling, energetic woman, full of life. Now she was like a helium balloon with a steady leak.

He opened the fridge, took out two bottles and twisted off the caps. He handed her one. "Let's sit." Pulling out the chair she'd used the night before, he waited until she took it before he sat down.

She sipped from the bottle, set it down and looked at him. "Mrs. Allred is retiring at the end of the year."

"She is?" He tried to process why that would affect Faye adversely. "Uh-oh. Is she sick? Does she have—"

"Nothing's wrong with her. I did ask that, eventually. She's retiring to spend more time with her husband."

"I can't remember who he— oh, wait. He owns the feed store."

"He does. I didn't remember that, either. He came to all the productions, though, was there every night, taking tickets, helping out with whatever." She took another swallow of her cider.

"Is *he* sick? Is that what's making you sad? She's retiring so she can nurse him through his final days?"

"Not at all. They're going to travel, probably in Europe." She gazed at him, her expression stony. "They want me to apply for her job."

His pulse leaped into the red zone. She could have a job here. His excitement died as quickly as it was born. Clearly she didn't want that job. "Who's *they*?"

"Mrs. Allred, the administration, the Wenches, probably your whole family if they hear about it. And mine. Mom and Dad supported my decision to make my home in Missoula, but if they thought there was a chance I'd come back here...."

The truth was a vise squeezing the air out of his lungs. She had an opportunity to teach theater and live in Wagon Train. It was the solution he'd been praying for and she was going to reject it. He could see it in her eyes.

She sighed. "I could be wrong, but I think you want me to take it, too. You lit up when I told you."

"I'll admit I got excited about it, but you aren't excited."

"No."

He controlled the urge to yell *why not? Mrs. Allred loved it and she's your idol!* But yelling wouldn't serve his cause. If he even had a cause anymore. "Why don't you want it?"

"Taking over from her would be an honor. But I already have a job I've made a huge commitment to. I'm eligible for tenure. I've built relationships with people in the department. I have a good reputation with the students. I can safely say they love me."

"Now that I totally believe."

"My leaving UM wouldn't have nearly the impact of Mrs. Allred leaving Wagon Train High, but it would have a negative impact. Not to mention they'd lose their grant writer."

"I remember that one. Everybody else strikes out."

"Oh, and the community theater has come to depend on me, too."

"UM and Missoula stand to lose a lot. I get that. But—"

"I know. Their loss is my high school's gain. And my family's."

"And mine."

Her breath hitched. "You don't know that."

"Yes, I do."

"You just think you do because we're living in a bubble. I'm not working so I'm free to spend time with you. There's nothing real about this week."

"I beg to differ. Making love with you is real. It's the most real thing I've done in years."

"But don't you see? When I'm involved in my work, I won't have time for that. I don't know how to multitask. I'm either working full tilt or diving into bed with you every five minutes. I can't do both."

"Who says?"

"I do! Every guy I've dated says I don't pay enough attention to him."

"Because none of them were right for you."

"I didn't give them a chance to be right. When it was a choice between them and work, I chose work."

"Not with me. You chose me."

"What do you mean? I'm not working this week."

"Of course you are. You're putting on a production for—"

"Not the same."

"It's exactly the same and when—"

"Gil, it's not. You haven't been there when I—"

"So it's not a full-scale production. You still had to choose between the rehearsal gig and being with me and you chose me, damn it."

"When?"

"When you were figuring out how to get the costumes repaired. You said you wouldn't let that cut into our time together."

She stared at him. "That's such a small—"

"But significant. Open your eyes, Faye. We have something special. You say you can't multitask but you can! You just need the right guy. You need me."

"And if it doesn't turn out like that? If I rip up my life and move down here and my pattern is just the same, what then?"

"It won't be the same! Trust me!"

"You're shouting."

He sucked in a breath. "I am. I'm sorry. It's just that I can see a beautiful life with you and I want you to see it, too."

"There's no way you can judge from this week, or more specifically, these couple of days. We haven't even spent the whole week together. You're seeing something that doesn't exist."

"It damn well does exist!" And he was shouting again.

"When I'm involved in a production, we work into the night, sometimes several nights in a row. Do you think I'll come home and make mad love to you when I'm exhausted?"

"I'm not saying that. We'll work it out. We'll find time because it will be important to both of us."

She crossed her arms over her chest. "You don't *get* it."

Something snapped deep inside. He threw up his hands in defeat. "You're right. I don't get why a beautiful, sexy, intelligent, funny, talented woman is convinced she's doomed to a life of work and no play."

"I didn't say—"

"Didn't you? That's what I heard. And I'm especially confused because this same woman has discovered the best sex of her life and the guy she had it with is begging her to give him a chance to prove she's *not* doomed to eternal celibacy."

"Are you done?"

"Yes, ma'am. I can either take you to bed or take you home. What'll it be?"

"Take me home."

Damn. That wasn't the answer he'd wanted. But at least she hadn't disputed his claim about the sex.

<u>**32**</u>

Faye didn't say anything on the drive back to her folks' house. Neither did Gil. She was running away, and he likely knew it. She tried to grab her suitcase before he did. He beat her to it and carried it to the porch. Then he tipped his hat and walked away.

Her mom met her at the door. Her dad was at the hospital with a patient in labor — not Penny, she quickly found out — so her mom was home alone. Typical of her, she didn't beat around the bush. "What happened?"

"Mrs. Allred's retiring this year, the school wants to give me her job and Gil thinks I should take it."

"Wow. And you had a fight about it?"

She nodded. "He has no idea what teaching theater is like. He thinks it would be like this week — some costume repair, one rehearsal, then the production. In between I could hang out with him. That's so unrealistic."

"I'm guessing you're not taking the job."

"I'm not. Sorry, Mom. You and Dad would probably love to have—"

"Sure, but not if you don't want it. You love what you're doing at UM. Why mess with something you've worked so hard for?"

"I know! Gil doesn't get that at all."

"Or he doesn't want to. Poor guy's in love with you. Probably has been ever since you were in the musical together."

"For ten years? No way."

"That's not so long, honey. And when you see the person again, it comes right back. It did for me and your dad."

"But that's you guys. You were supposed to be together. Gil's just... I don't know what he is. Obtuse. Extremely obtuse."

"Love can do that to a person. Did you eat?"

"Didn't get around to that."

"I was about to warm up some leftover lasagna if you're interested."

"Sounds good. Thanks. I'll set the table." She wasn't hungry, but saying so would make her sound lovesick. Which she wasn't. She was mad.

Unfortunately, she couldn't be mad at the Wenches. They'd thought she'd want to know. And they'd likely hoped for a different reaction. She couldn't be mad at Gil. He was in love with her, so much in love that he refused to listen. What she said didn't align with his fantasy.

That left being mad at herself. She was the one who'd suggested this *indulgence*. Of course Gil had said yes. She was as guilty of self-delusion as he was. Everyone had predicted it wouldn't work. They'd all been right. Now what?

The answer was obvious. The show must go on.

* * *

When Faye woke up in her childhood twin bed on Wednesday morning, she couldn't figure out why she was there. Once she did, she remembered the garment bags. And her costume, which she'd left hanging in Gil's closet, along with his T-shirt and the pants with a compromised zipper.

So much for stalking off in a huff. The zipper might just need to be rubbed with a bar of soap. Or her lip balm. The garment bag situation wasn't so simple. Gil and his truck had figured prominently in her plan for this production.

She'd envisioned they'd use his truck to transport the garment bags to Rowdy Roost Thursday night and into town on Friday. The bags could stay safely locked in the truck during the rehearsal, then taken to the Buffalo for the show, and afterward hauled back to her parents' house, where they'd stay until Sunday when she returned them to Mrs. Allred.

Great plan. Too bad she'd torpedoed it by choosing to have him take her home instead of to bed. But she'd made the right choice, even if it complicated the costume transport.

Okay, she could handle this. All of it. She'd drive out this afternoon when he was at the shop, fix his zipper and grab her costumes, both for *Summer Nights* and *You're the One That I Want.* She'd leave him a note saying she'd be back Thursday night to help him load the garment bags in his truck.

By Thursday night she'd have her game face on. She'd keep it there until the wedding reception ended. Who said drama classes were fluff? Thanks to her training, she'd breeze right through the next four days and emerge without a scratch.

Her mom had left for work and had scribbled a note on the family chalkboard. *Dad's asleep. Let me know if you'll be here for dinner. Love, Mom*

She'd drawn a little heart at the end of the message. Faye gazed at it, emotion clogging her throat. The familiar handwriting, the heart, even the chalkboard that had hung in the kitchen all her life had more significance this morning.

Refusing the job at Wagon Train High made sense in so many ways, but there was no getting around it. She missed her family. Getting to see them more often would have been nice.

After she'd announced she wouldn't be taking the job, her mother hadn't mentioned it again. Would she love having both her daughters close? Of course. Would she push that agenda? Never.

She reread the message. *Dad's asleep.* That sort of thing happened a lot with his job. Her mother could have pointed out that his long hours hadn't ruined their marriage. But she hadn't gone into that, hadn't tried to interfere.

Picking up the chalk, Faye wrote under her mom's message. *Dinner's on me. I'll bring home burgers from the Buffalo. Love, Faye.* She added several hearts, swallowed a lump in her throat and put down the chalk.

Then she texted Mrs. Allred, asking for some of her time this morning. Her drama teacher and friend deserved to hear the news from the source.

A few more vehicles occupied the high school parking lot than had been there on Monday. A slight chill in the air and a whiff of smoke from someone's fireplace signaled that fall was on its way. Her favorite time of year. The start of school.

Mrs. Allred had said to meet her on the auditorium stage, where she was playing around with the new curtain that had been installed the day before.

A wave of nostalgia hit Faye when she walked into the empty auditorium, her footsteps echoing as she walked across the floor and up the steps to the stage. The smell of floor wax was the same, but the mustiness had been replaced by the sharp scent of new fabric.

Gone was the faded maroon curtain that had hung across the stage when she'd performed on it. Its replacement was a rich forest green.

"Mrs. Allred?"

The curtain separated and then whooshed open quickly as her drama teacher pulled vigorously on the ropes. "Isn't it *glorious*?" She spread her arms. "Finally! The curtain of my dreams!" She corralled her mane of curly gray hair and anchored it with a scrunchie she pulled from her pocket.

"Is it a going away present from the school board?"

"It's a welcome present for the new drama teacher."

Her chest hurt. "Mrs. Allred, I'm not—"

"I know, sweetheart. I could tell from the tone of your text. That's fine. I knew it was a long shot." She walked across the stage as if she owned it. Everyone in town would agree she did. "When I heard about you and Gil, I wondered if that would help my cause or hurt it."

"It's not really about Gil."

"My darling girl." She caught both of Faye's hands and squeezed them. "It's always been about Gil."

She gulped. "If you're talking about my silly crush ten years ago...."

"It wasn't silly and it wasn't a crush. He was your first love and you were his. And he broke your tender heart, which is what eighteen-year-old boys are famous for."

"So true. I'm thankful I'm not that girl anymore."

Mrs. Allred's gaze softened. "I've known you a long time, Faye. I have nothing but admiration for what you've accomplished. You've worked like a demon, not wasting a single moment."

"Because I love what I do. And as you know, the rewards are huge."

"They are, impossible to quantify." She released Faye's hands and swept an arm toward the stage. "I've lived a thousand lives here. I've watched my children — and I think of them as mine — pretend to be someone else. It expands their world, takes them closer to becoming full-fledged adults. It's magic."

"Yes, it is." Gil had used that word.

"And magic is the best word to describe the connection between you and Gil. When I saw it on stage, it took my breath away."

Faye stood in stunned silence. Where was she going with this? Why even bring it up?

"I've seen how you've avoided him all these years and I don't blame you. He wounded you and you were afraid he'd do it again. But he left a hole in your heart, and... I say this with love... you've been trying to fill it with work."

She stiffened. "*No.* No, I haven't. He has nothing to do with my career. *Nothing.* And he doesn't understand it *at all*, which is why I can't be with him." She searched her drama teacher's expression for a frown of uncertainty, lifted eyebrows, anything to signal that she understood that much at least.

Instead she smiled. "You'd be taking a risk, a big risk, if you let yourself love him again, but oh, Faye, the possibilities." Her eyes sparkled. "You two...." She paused and took a breath. "You could set the world on fire."

33

All day Thursday Gil waited for Faye's text announcing she was calling off the performance. Sure, she'd fixed his pants and left a note saying she'd be there to help load the garment bags at six-thirty for the rehearsal at Rowdy Roost. But, c'mon. Was she really going to put them through this?

Apparently so. By six-fifteen he faced facts. That stubborn woman would arrive on his doorstep as promised. They would rehearse with the gang and perform at the Buffalo on Friday night, come hell or high water.

Hell was a guarantee. The way things were going, a flood could come along at any minute. He'd welcome it with open arms. Heading into his bedroom, he put on his outfit.

He'd just finished pulling up the zipper on his pants, which she had indeed improved a hundred percent, when she rapped on the front door. "Come in!"

Damn, he was hoarse. He cleared his throat. Would his voice fail him? That would suck the big one. Or maybe he'd fall down while he was dancing because he was distracted by the fustercluck this had turned into. *Fustercluck.* One of her words. Yeah, she'd haunt him forever.

When he walked back into his living room, Sandy, aka the bane of his existence, stood waiting for him, this time in a poodle skirt and fifties-style blouse. His stupid heart started pounding with joy. *Joy.* He was so messed up it wasn't even funny.

"Did you get a chance to talk with Bret?"

"I did, and he took the whole thing better than I thought he would. He agreed I'd be miserable in New York or LA."

"That must be a relief. Are you gonna start dancing around the shop?"

He rolled his eyes.

"Well, you could, now that Bret's been informed."

"Dancing while welding isn't recommended."

"That's not what I meant and you know it. You're just pulling my chain. As usual."

"Is that a crack? Because if we're going to start trading insults, we really can't go through with—"

"Sorry." She waved her hands, palms out. "Let's start over. Thank you for being willing to perform with me. I told Ella that we parted amicably because I didn't want her to think we were forcing ourselves to do this."

He filled his lungs with some very necessary air. "I'm afraid I didn't give Bret that same impression. I warned him the performance might not happen, after all."

"Why wouldn't it?"

"Because your two lead singers aren't getting along? How about that?"

"Since when is that a reason to cancel a performance? Everybody else is looking forward to it, especially the bunch waiting for us at your mom's place. They've all been practicing the song, doing the work."

"I know. And by the way, Bret's the only one I've told that we've split. I asked him to keep it to himself."

"You haven't said anything to your mom?"

"No. Then again, I haven't seen anyone in the family except Bret. Your folks must know, since you're back there."

"They do."

"And what did they say?"

Her gaze skittered away. "That I needed to do what I thought was best."

"That's it?"

"Pretty much."

There was more or she'd look him in the eye. But what Liz and Doc Bradley thought wasn't of much consequence. They'd leave the matter up to her and he went along with that program. But it would be nice to think he had allies.

"We should get those bags loaded."

"Yes, ma'am." He paused. "I could have done it without you."

"You could have, but I promised Mrs. Allred I'd be personally responsible for these costumes, which in my mind means I'll be present whenever they're being moved from one place to another. That might sound a little OCD, but—"

"I get it. I was just checking. That means you'll come back out here tomorrow afternoon when they need to be taken into town?"

"I was planning on it."

"Well, here's a thought. Feel free to reject it if you want. I'll be closing up the shop early and coming back here to get those costumes. You could ride out with me. That way your car doesn't end up sitting at the ranch for however long until you have a chance to fetch it."

She hesitated. "I hadn't thought that through." Then she nodded. "Thank you. That would be helpful."

"One other thing. Are we just rehearsing *Summer Nights*? Or both? For that matter, are we even doing the other one?"

She blinked. "I checked with Tyra and the band can play both, so I was planning on doing the other one. Unless you don't want to."

Ah. So he'd get to decide. He could say no and she couldn't very well make him. But now that she was standing here, he could feel the zing of connection even though he wasn't touching her.

If they danced *You're the One That I Want*, touching was part of it. Sucker that he was, he wanted that. "Let's do both numbers."

"But we don't have to rehearse the second one tonight."

"Good." Except now he wanted to.

* * *

Friday turned out to be a gorgeous day, which just seemed wrong to Gil, who was tied up into one big ol' knot of frustration. The rehearsal had been barrels of fun… for everybody except him.

But he'd faked it until his jaw nearly locked up on him from all the forced grins. Shades of the party last Saturday night, except this was worse, because he and Faye were supposed to be getting along like two peas in a pod.

He had to give the devil her due. Faye was way better at acting than he was. She covered for him several times, and near as he could tell, the gang had no idea the relationship had crumbled like a two-week-old slice of wedding cake.

And now, because he was an idiot, he'd offered to drive her out to the ranch to save her gas and extra trouble. A glutton for punishment. He should have that engraved on his tombstone.

She came out the door the minute he pulled up. Wouldn't you just know she'd look amazing? She rarely wore a dress and this one had daisies all over it. He loved daisies.

He hopped out and rounded the truck in time to help her in. "Pretty dress."

"Thanks." She let him hand her in. Even gave him a tentative smile. "This is very nice of you."

"I'm a very nice guy." He closed the door and jogged around to the driver's side, the weight on his chest not quite as heavy. She'd thrown him a crumb and he'd gobbled it right up.

He fastened his seatbelt and started the truck. "Don't let me forget to feed Sam while we're there. Mom asked me to do that since she's already at the church helping set up."

"I'll remind you."

"Thanks." He'd turned the radio off on the way over and he left it off. Music was a touchy subject. Instead he picked a neutral one. "Looks like Penny's going to make it through the wedding."

"Sure does. Through the *Summer Nights* number, too. My dad thinks she's got another week at least."

"Since he's the father of the bride, I hope he's right."

"Ella knew she was taking a chance having her wedding around the same time the babies were due. So far, she's lucked out."

"Is she nervous?"

"About the babies?"

"About getting married."

"Are you kidding? She's marrying her best friend. If any couple is bullet-proof, they are."

"Still, it's a big commitment. *As long as you both shall live.* That's powerful stuff."

"I know." She said it quietly.

Time to get off that subject. He couldn't even say why he'd felt the need to broach it. Except they were a day away from his brother's wedding.

No matter how bonded two people were, it was still a little intimidating to consider the ramifications of those vows. The only woman who would make him think seriously about saying those words was sitting next to him and she had zero interest in being a major player in his life.

"I went to see Mrs. Allred Wednesday morning."

"You did?" She startled him with that one. Why tell him?

"I wanted to explain in person why I wouldn't be taking the job."

"She probably appreciated that."

"The stage has a new curtain, forest green."

"That's great. The old one was garbage. Too bad she'll only enjoy it for a year, though."

"Yeah. She... um..." She cleared her throat. "She thinks you're the reason I'm not taking the job."

His breath hitched. Sure, he might be part of the reason, but not the whole reason. "What gives her that idea?"

"She thinks it all goes back to the musical and whatever happened after that."

"You told her?"

"Of course not!"

He heaved a sigh of relief.

"But she thinks I'm still stuck on you and that's why I work so hard."

"What?"

"Gil, slow down. You're doing eighty."

He eased off on the gas but there wasn't much he could do about his racing heart. "Where is she getting that stuff?"

"She says I'm filling the hole you left in my heart."

The words gut-punched him. Swerving off the road, he braked the truck and turned to her. "That's not true. Please tell me—"

"It's not true. I love what I do. But..." Her brow wrinkled. "Remember what I said about the community theater Halloween project? That I volunteered because it would give me an out for the five-year-reunion?"

"Yeah. But you said the play was fun."

"It was, but my motivation was avoiding you, making sure I didn't have to see you there with a girlfriend."

"That would have bothered you?"

"Yes, dammit. Which makes me a terrible person. I'm afraid to get involved with you, but I don't want anyone else to, either."

"Hang on. You're *afraid* to get involved with me?"

She nodded.

"Why?"

"Because you'll find out I'm no fun when I'm working and you'll… leave."

"Oh, Faye." He reached for her.

She backed away and held up a hand. "You can say that won't happen, but it *could* happen."

The weight was back on his chest, heavier than ever. "In other words, you don't believe in me." He swallowed. "I put that hole in your heart and I could add another one."

"Could be."

"Is there anything I can do or say that would make a difference?"

She gazed at him, confusion and sorrow clouding her gray eyes. "I don't think so."

He wanted to howl in despair. If only he could time-travel back ten years and fix what he'd broken. Since that wasn't an option, he put the truck in gear and drove to Rowdy Ranch.

34

Faye had nothing more to say after that and silence was preferable to idle chit-chat. Gil likely felt the same, since he kept quiet, too.

They loaded the garment bags with a minimum of communication. She reminded him about feeding Sam, and they headed back to town.

Gil's breathing was steady, but he wasn't at ease. Every so often his thumb would tap, tap, tap on the steering wheel. His tight jaw and the furrow between his eyebrows signaled a troubled man.

Her doing. An apology was in order. "I just made things worse. I'm sorry."

"I'm glad you said something. At least I know what I'm up against."

"But there's nothing you can do. It's my issue."

"I'm the one who helped create it. On top of that, I could have been more proactive way earlier. The first time I realized you were avoiding me, which was years ago, I could have taken action."

"Like what? Drag me off by my hair? I didn't want to talk to you and I made sure that wasn't ever going to happen."

"Until Saturday night."

"I'd let my guard down. The party was over. I was on my way out the door. You bushwhacked me."

"I suppose I did. And in spite of everything, I don't regret it."

"You did the right thing. We have a shot at being friends, now."

"I sure hope so. Your dad does, too."

"When did he say that?"

"After we discussed the gate."

"Did he warn you not to break my heart or else?"

"He said he could make that speech since that was what I expected, but since he knows his daughter, he figured we were equally at risk."

"He thought I might break your heart?"

"Yes, ma'am."

Her breath caught. "Have I?"

"Not yet. It's a little dinged up, but it doesn't feel like it's broken."

"Maybe we called a halt just in time."

He glanced at her. "We'll see."

* * *

Thursday night's rehearsal had been a slog. As the person who'd organized the performance, Faye had felt responsible for keeping the mood positive even when she was in turmoil.

But the wedding rehearsal was a different matter. While she had a role as the maid of honor, she wasn't the person in charge. Besides, she'd learned the routine a year ago for Ella's wedding that never happened.

She'd suspected that one would be a disaster, but this one had success written all over it. The wedding party was large and boisterous, great camouflage for her constantly shifting emotions.

It included Marsh's brothers minus Cheyenne on the groom's side. The bride's attendants were Faye, Brit and Ella's future sisters-in-law minus Kendall. The proud parents of Josephine Desiree would watch the wedding at home on Cheyenne's phone while Dallas streamed it live from his phone tomorrow.

Since Faye's duties were minor, she fell into an old habit — watching Gil McLintock work a room. A week ago she'd seen confidence bordering on arrogance. Now she saw both chinks in his armor and his inner strength.

He'd forced the issue last Saturday night when she'd been willing to let it continue indefinitely. He'd allowed himself to be vulnerable this week. So had she. Especially during their last exchange.

She hadn't planned to tell him about her conversation with Mrs. Allred. But she'd been thinking about it ever since Wednesday morning. Once they were enclosed in the intimacy of his truck cab, the words had spilled out.

Confessing her deepest fear had loosened her tension but transferred it to him. He joked around with his brothers as usual but every so often his smile would fade and he'd stare into space. In those moments she longed to go to him, hold him close and tell him... what? *That you love him, dummy.*

And then what? Admit she'd spent ten years denying it? That she'd built a life in Missoula and crammed it with unceasing work to avoid the pain? Could she even say that out loud let alone to him? Not now.

The rehearsal didn't take long and neither did the drive to the Buffalo. Fortunately they needed to discuss the game plan for the coming performance and didn't get into anything personal.

As they unloaded the garment bags and carried them back to Clint and Tyra's office, Faye slipped into her director's role. She'd chosen to present the two numbers during happy hour to minimize the danger of food getting on the costumes.

The band set up and played a few tunes while Faye passed out costumes. Thanks to assistance from Tyra and Clint, everyone was dressed in a relatively short time.

It was a motley crew, with most of the gang going for a laugh more than authenticity. Especially Penny. She fastened the waist of her poodle skirt just under her breasts, empire-style. She'd opted for only one crinoline since her skirt already had volume courtesy of her baby bump.

Originally Faye had imagined doing *Summer Nights* on the stage, but after last night 's practice she'd decided they'd be better off on the dance floor. She and Gil would have cordless mics they could point at their backup singers when needed.

The guys clearly loved their black leather jackets. They'd all popped the collars and swaggered around, a gathering of wannabe tough guys.

Faye picked up the mics from the stage and gave one to Gil. So many members of the wedding party were performing that the audience was small, but highly engaged.

They'd claimed tables at the edge of the dance floor—her folks, Desiree and Andy, Buck and Marybeth. Mrs. Allred had come with her husband Jim and the two Wenches who had spouses had brought them along. Technically Bret was in charge of Zach and Maverick, but with so many grandma and grandpa figures around, he didn't have much to do.

After announcing the number, Faye took one last glance at the ensemble and signaled the band.

Gil gave her a wink, a typical Danny Zuco move, and started to sing.

Her heart swelled as it always did when he sang. Joy swirled through her as she joined her voice with his. The invisible cord that connected them when they shared a stage snapped into place.

They played to the audience and they played to each other. Their backup singers outdid themselves. No one muffed a single line. When she and Gil met at center stage and blended their voices for the song's ending, their audience made up in volume what they lacked in size, clapping and stomping their feet.

Gil grabbed her hand and they executed their bow, the same one they'd done in the waiting room of the hospital. Then they gestured to their backup singers, which generated more loud applause from their appreciative spectators.

When the noise died down, Faye spoke into her mic. "Thank you so much. Time for the costumes to go back in the bags, gang. Gil and I will do a quick change and be back for an extra number, our version of *You're the One That I Want.*"

More cheers followed that announcement.

Turning off the mics and laying them on the bandstand, she and Gil headed into the chaos surrounding the office and the bathrooms. She managed to carve out a space for herself in the bathroom.

Gil only had to switch his white *Summer Nights* T-shirt for the black one. He'd decided to substitute his green and gold letterman's jacket for the white Rydell High letter sweater in the garment bag. She appreciated the gesture since the script called for him to throw that white sweater on the ground.

He was waiting for her when she came out of the bathroom. "Great job on *Summer Nights,* by the way."

"You, too."

They walked together out to the dance floor. This time Gil picked up the mics and handed hers over with a bow. She blew him a kiss, which brought a whistle from somebody, probably Beau.

Backing away, she struck a pose as the band played the opening. Gil exaggerated his reaction as if he'd just caught sight of her. Ripping off his jacket, he tossed it to the floor and launched into the song, exaggerating his hip action even more than he had in his living room.

His family *loved* it, almost drowning him out with cheers and whistles. When he slid to his knees at her feet, they rattled the rafters.

She gulped back laughter and managed to stay in character, nudging him with her foot.

He glanced up, his blue eyes sparkling.

And she sang to him, using words she didn't have the courage to say when they were alone. But for now, she could be Sandy, a girl with a happy-ever-after ending with her Danny. She danced her heart out as they created the electricity that had taken Mrs. Allred's breath away.

The magic spread throughout the room and the group rose to its feet as everyone sang the familiar chorus. When she jumped into his arms for the last few bars of the song and he whirled her around, the crowd was singing so loud that she and Gil didn't have to.

They were a hit. Smiling, she met his gaze. And went still. As she looked into his eyes, her world shifted. There was no mistaking the depth of emotion shining there.

Then his lips moved. *I love you.* The song ended.

He set her on her feet and kissed her, a quick, firm press of lips before he caught her hand and turned so they could make their traditional bow to a wildly cheering audience. Leaving their seats, everyone poured onto the dance floor,

She squeezed his hand as the crowd closed in. What had just happened? They'd never discussed the subject of love. Not ten years ago and not this week.

Sure, others had said he loved her. She'd even mentally acknowledged that he probably did. But since he'd never said the words and neither had she, the subject had been shoved under the bed.

Until now. Looked like they wouldn't slide slowly into platonic friendship, after all. He'd put his heart on the line.

35

Terrible timing. Gil cursed himself for a fool. Why had he felt the need to tell Faye he loved her in the middle of a crowd? Had he imagined she'd say it back and drag him off to some private spot where they could seal the deal with ravenous kisses?

Clearly that wasn't gonna happen. Might never happen. She'd been avoiding him ever since they'd left the dance floor.

But she'd have to talk to him before the night was over. They had to reload the garment bags in his truck and transport them to her folks' house. He'd use that time to clean up the mess he'd made.

Wouldn't be too much longer before they needed to collect those bags. The group had started to disperse.

Then Jim Allred sought him out. "Hey, Gil, that was some fancy dancing out there, son."

"Thanks, Mr. Allred."

"Carolyn says you must be putting in some serious practice time. Either that or you're more of a prodigy than she thought."

"I'm no prodigy, sir. I've been practicing."

"It shows. Anyway, just wanted you to know you don't have to worry about those costumes. Carolyn and I will take them off your hands and get 'em back in storage. I was supposed to tell you earlier but I forgot."

"You have a vehicle that will handle all that?"

"My work truck is plenty big enough. That's why we drove it over here. Carolyn figured with the wedding and all, you two don't need to be bothering with the costumes. We're glad to help out."

"But..." Gil frantically searched for a reason why he and Faye needed to follow the original plan. "I'm sure Faye wants to clean some things before she gives them back to you."

"She did say something about that, but she's also given Carolyn a donation for the drama department. We'll take care of getting things cleaned."

Gil thanked Jim for his generosity. The costumes belonged to the school and if the person in charge of them wanted to take them back herself, she certainly could. Which meant he wouldn't get that time alone with Faye, after all.

As he mulled over the possibility of asking her to step outside for a moment so they could talk, she showed up. "I'm going home with Mom and Dad. Just wanted to let you know."

He swallowed. "I think we need to—"

"We do." She laid a hand on his chest. "We will. Tomorrow. See you then." She gave him a quick kiss on the cheek and went over to join her parents.

Well, that settled it. She was done with him. A peck on the cheek? That's how you treated the guy you were dumping. He was so dumped.

Might as well say his goodbyes and drive home, too. The hell of it was, he couldn't drink until he puked. He had to be bright and shiny for the wedding tomorrow. He owed it to Marsh and Ella.

* * *

Since this was the fifth time Gil had stood up for one of his brothers' weddings, logically it should be old hat by now. Except he'd never been in a wedding with Faye.

Technically he should be exhausted. He and his brothers had spent the morning pulling tables and chairs out of Rowdy Roost and into the front yard to create an outdoor venue for the reception. If the northern lights made an appearance as Ella hoped, she and the guests would have a perfect view.

But it wasn't exhaustion that claimed him as he stood between Sky and Beau at the altar listening to Taylor Swift's *Fearless*. Anticipation at seeing Faye had him by the throat. When she appeared at the end of the carpeted aisle in her teal maid of honor dress, he gulped.

She'd said she was afraid to be with him, afraid that when he discovered the real her, he'd leave. How could he let her know he knew the real her so well, she'd be shocked at the depth of it?

He'd been watching her since he was eighteen. In the years when he'd had to duck out of sight when she appeared in the distance, he hadn't walked away. He'd spied on her, memorizing the way she walked, the tilt of her head, how she laughed, the shape of her smile.

Without understanding why, he'd picked up hints of what she was up to from bits and pieces dropped by Ella during family gatherings. Faye hadn't been there, but she'd been discussed.

In the few times she had been at events, he'd soaked up the sight of her without admitting to himself he was doing it. And now... as she came toward him down the aisle, he kept his attention on her face, trying to gauge her mood. Was she looking at him?

Yes. Hope leaped in his pathetic heart. She was looking right at him. Oh, God, was he imagining what he was seeing in those beautiful gray eyes? He was perfectly capable of delusional thinking.

Her sweet mouth tilted in a soft smile. Was she smiling at *him*? Sure seemed like it. *Breathe, dude.*

Then she broke eye contact. Logically she had to since she'd come to the end of the aisle. She walked over to her spot, pivoted and faced the back of the church. Turning her head in his direction would've been weird. He wanted her to, anyway.

When she didn't, his heart rate became almost normal. He could have imagined that she was deliberately focusing on him and that her smile had been a signal of some kind. Her peck on the cheek last night still stung.

The Taylor Swift song was eerily appropriate since it was about a woman who finds the courage to love a guy. He hadn't paid attention to the lyrics during the rehearsal. Too busy trying to act like he was fine, just fine.

But after the way she'd looked at him on her way down the aisle, his nerves were doing a slow burn. His skin prickled.

The music switched to *You're Still the One* by Shania Twain and Ella appeared in all her glory, one arm linked through her mother's and the other through her father's. Tall and athletic, she hardly ever dressed up. Today she was covered in delicate white lace.

Gil snuck a look at Marsh. His brother was clearly having a religious experience gazing at his bride walking slowly toward him.

Didn't take much imagination for Gil to put himself in Marsh's place and Faye in Ella's. Ten minutes ago he wouldn't have liked his chances. But that little smile....

Ella joined Marsh at the altar and her parents took their seats. The minister welcomed the guests and said a few words about marriage.

Gil listened harder than he ever had as the blood pounded through his veins. He needed to understand the implications of this ceremony. Just in case.

Then the minister paused and Faye stepped out of the line of attendants, a mic in her hand.

Gil braced himself for another emotional hit as Faye sang *When You Say Nothing at All.* He loved that song, and her rendition was better than any he'd heard. Then again, she could sing the alphabet and he'd close his eyes and ride that voice to paradise.

When she finished, Beau's elbow jarred him back to reality.

"Hey, Captain Obvious," his brother muttered.

No doubt. The ceremony continued as Ella and Marsh spoke the vows they'd written. Gil absorbed them in a way he hadn't with any of the other four weddings. Was Faye listening, too?

And then it was done. Amid cheering from the guests, Ella and Marsh headed back down the aisle to Ryan Hurd's *Diamonds or Twine.*

Sky stepped forward to escort Faye and Gil followed with Brit. He concentrated on paying attention to Brit while every cell in his body vibrated because he was only steps away from Faye.

Sky's truck was the first in the line of trucks in front of the church. Ella and Marsh were already in the back seat when Sky helped Faye into the front.

Gil handed Brit into the passenger seat of his truck as Beau and Jess took the backseat. Having Beau in his vehicle meant not having to make conversation. Beau filled any and all gaps, for which he was grateful.

But when, oh, when would he have a chance to talk with Faye? Not during the picture-taking. That became clear once they arrived at the ranch where the photographer was already set up.

She made use of the porch, the barn, even the corral. The process dragged on through various combinations of wedding party folks. Hardly any left Gil and Faye out of the shot at the same time, and when they did she was always in deep conversation with someone else.

That finally ended when it was too dark to make picture-taking viable. The band reclaimed the porch, drinks were served, and the bride and groom took the floor for their first dance. They'd requested Luke Combs' *Forever After All.*

Time to make a move. Gil stepped close to Faye and slipped his fingers through hers. She kept her gaze on her sister and Marsh twirling around the floor, but she gripped his hand.

His breath hitched. He stood with her, heart skipping around like a hummingbird in a field of flowers. Her fingers slowly tightened on his.

When the song ended, Ella invited everyone out on the floor. The band struck up Thomas Rhett's *Die a Happy Man.*

Gil opened his mouth to invite Faye to dance, then closed it as she tugged him out on the floor and settled into his arms. It was a deliciously slow song with a sensuous beat. If she dumped him after this, that would be cold, but he'd give her points for class.

Winding her arms around his neck, she lifted her face, her gaze soft. Then she mouthed the words that he'd dreamed of, three words that he'd given up all hope of ever hearing from her. Technically, he still hadn't heard them. Then again, neither had she last night.

He stopped dancing. "You do?"

She nodded. "Keep dancing."

He shuffled his feet but stayed in one place.

Her smile bloomed. "Is that the best you can do?"

"Yes, ma'am. Could we maybe go—"

"Sure." Slipping out of his arms, she took his hand. "Follow me."

"Anywhere." He was curious where she'd take him. Into the house? Behind the barn?

She led him through the tables and out toward the corral, but she bypassed that and headed for the pasture gate. Lifting the latch, she pushed it open and stepped through.

It was empty since the horses were in for the night. The moon was now half-full, creating a pale swath of light on the fragrant grass under their feet. A soft breeze carried music and laughter toward them, but it was muted, not loud enough to block the chirp of crickets.

After taking several steps, Faye turned to him. "How's this?"

"Better." He cleared his throat. "Would you mind repeating what you said back there? Only out loud?"

"After you do the same with what you said last night."

Then he got it. Pulling her close, he took a deep breath. "I love you."

Sighing, she snuggled against him. "I love you, too, you crazy man. And it looks like you're stuck with me. I called Mrs. Allred this morning and took the job."

"You took—" He choked up, had to clear his throat again. "Really?"

"We'll have a messy year between now and next May. Lots of driving back and forth."

"I'll drive 'til the tires on my truck go bald. But what changed your mind?"

"It's been changing. Especially after I talked to Mrs. Allred. She's right. It's always been about you. I've used *so* much energy convincing myself I *didn't* want you. But… you're the one that I want."

"Except if you're afraid I'll leave…."

"Which I was. Then you did this brave thing. You said you love me."

"Not out loud, though and the timing was horrible. I should never have—"

"Your timing was perfect. I was still scared, and then you handed me your heart to cherish or to smash. That took guts. And because I knew what you were risking, I believed you. You love me."

"So much."

"Then I have no reason to be scared."

"No reason at all." Cupping her cheek, he held her gaze, ready to take one more giant leap into the unknown. "I have something to ask."

"You want me to spend weekends at your cabin and I'll do the best that I—"

"Marry me."

"Doggone it! That's my line!"

"Huh?"

"I was going to ask *you*." She reached into the V-neck of her dress and pulled out his class ring. "Gil McLintock, will you marry me?"

Slaphappy with joy, he started laughing. Life with Faye was going to be one hell of a ride. "You're proposing by giving my ring back?"

"Oh. Hm. I see your point. It sounded better in my head."

"The answer is yes. Yes, I'll marry you. I'll even wear this ring on a chain around my neck. But right now I desperately need to kiss you."

"Good, because I desperately need you to do that."

"Then come here, you." He started off gently, his heart hammering. This was it. The moment he'd—

"*Oh! Look, everybody! Look, look!*"

With a groan of impatience, he lifted his head and gazed at her. "Don't tell me they're watching us."

She smiled. "Not this time."

"Then what...." He followed the direction of her gaze. Iridescent shades of green, blue and white danced in the night sky. "*Oh.*"

She sighed. "It's magical."

"So are we."

She turned from the lights and looked up at him, her eyes glowing with love. "I know."

Lowering his head, he touched his lips to hers in a kiss he would remember forever. Life with Faye, a life filled with magic, had begun.

New York Times bestselling author Vicki Lewis Thompson's love affair with cowboys started with the Lone Ranger, continued through Maverick, and took a turn south of the border with Zorro. She views cowboys as the Western version of knights in shining armor, rugged men who value honor, honesty and hard work. Fortunately for her, she lives in the Arizona desert, where broad-shouldered, lean-hipped cowboys abound. Blessed with such an abundance of inspiration, she only hopes that she can do them justice.

For more information about this prolific author, visit her website and sign up for her newsletter. She loves connecting with readers.

VickiLewisThompson.com